O9-BUD-702

3 5674 05666682 0

The Dopeman's Wife

Part 1 of the

Dopeman's Trilogy

SHERWOOD FOREST LIBRARY
7117 W. 7 MILE RD.
DETROIT, MI 48221

APR   2017

SF

The Dopeman's Wife

Part 1 of the

Dopeman's Trilogy

JaQuavis Coleman

www.urbanbooks.net

Urban Books, LLC
97 N18th Street
Wyandanch, NY 11798

The Dopeman's Wife: Part 1 of the Dopeman's Trilogy
© Copyright 2009 JaQuavis Coleman

All rights reserved. No part of this book may be reproduced in any form or by any means without prior consent of the Publisher, excepting brief quotes used in reviews.

ISBN 13: 978-1-60162-626-4
ISBN 10:1-60162-626-6

First Mass Market Printing November 2011
First Trade Paperback Printing May 2009
Printed in the United States of America

10 9 8 7 6 5 4 3

This is a work of fiction. Any references or similarities to actual events, real people, living, or dead, or to real locales are intended to give the novel a sense of reality. Any similarity in other names, characters, places, and incidents is entirely coincidental.

Distributed by Kensington Publishing Corp.
Submit Wholesale Orders to:
Kensington Publishing Corp.
C/O Penguin Group (USA) Inc.
Attention: Order Processing
405 Murray Hill Parkway
East Rutherford, NJ 07073-2316
Phone: 1-800-526-0275
Fax: 1-800-227-9604

Acknowledgments

First I want to thank the Creator for inspiring me to create these novels and giving me the gift of a vast imagination. It's a blessing to have the ability to paint pictures with words, and I am forever grateful. I want to thank my gorgeous wife for being my backbone and being my number one hater, LOL. I'm the best writer in the house! All bullshit aside, you are my inspiration and my favorite author, and I am proud of everything you do.

THANKS to Carl Weber for mentoring and being a friend. No, for being family. You have kept it 100 since the first day I met you in Detroit, and I appreciate realness. You taught me how to get to the money.

Thanks to Natalie Weber for putting up with all my calls and questions. You are a wonderful person, and I am glad to have the privilege of working with you. Denard Breland, thanks for being real and family. Also shout-outs to Martha

Weber. To Keisha Ervin, Silk, Jarold Imes, Erick Gray, Torrian Ferguson, Mark Anthony, and Michelle Moore. A big thanks to G-Unit Books and Ian Kleinart. What up, Liz!! To Amaleka McCall, you are 'bout to blow, watch!! Shout-outs to my lawyer Harold Millhouse for beating those cases on my behalf; I owe you.

I would like to thank the city of Flint for giving me the life experiences and circumstances to pen these tales authentically. This is a message to the Flint Police Department: I DO NOT LIVE WHAT I WRITE ABOUT, SO LET ME LIVE. Thanks to Janay Coleman, Kamela Dixon, SHAY (my baby), Johnny Davis, Shelton Jones, Pooh Jay, Lil Recco, K. Gardin and TRE (one of my closest friends in life), FATRAT, Dotta (my brother), Jon and Christine Love, Sydney, India, Jazz, Mario, Jackie Hill, Cali, Tanya Jones, Margo, Lavelle Crump, Dorothy Crump, Shawna, Izzy, Amir, Jalen, Shawn South, Retta, Kim (Lady Scorpio), Glam, Virgo, Mistic, Token, Tazzyt2Bossy, The Reading Rendezvous, Toni (OOSA), Ebony, Lonnie, Anari, Ernest, Aunt Lean, Debra Thames, Quanisha, Tammy, Tony T, Chloe, Veronica, Denise Weatherspoon, Courtney, Unk Larry, Aunt Mo-Ink, Mike at Supreme Styles, Gabe, Dominae, and Lil Nique, Mr. and Mrs. Johnnie Coleman, Johnnie Coleman JR (OG) and Mr. and Mrs.

Webster. Shout-out to my hood the Fifth Ward and all its soldiers. Jake, Naldo . . . Keep holding me down, y'all niggas my brothers 'til death. B-Block my other home: Blaze, Dunna, Pipes, 40, Quinn. Bridget Summerville (mama), and Frenchie. Can't forget Lil Douggie—Hold ya head behind them walls. I hope my stories can provide you a brief escape. R.I.P AC, R.I.P. HEAD. Thanks to all my fans and readers. I appreciate all of the support, e-mails, and love that I get from you guys. THANK YOU! I can be reached at:

quavo_writer@yahoo.com
or
www.myspace.com/ quavo_writer1

And to my Jersey plug . . . I would never mention ya name.
Enjoy my story.
ONE

But the allure of the game, keeps calling your name To all the Lauras of the world, I feel your pain To all the Christies in every cities and Tiffany Lanes We all hustlers in love with the same thing . . . It's just the life

—Jay-Z

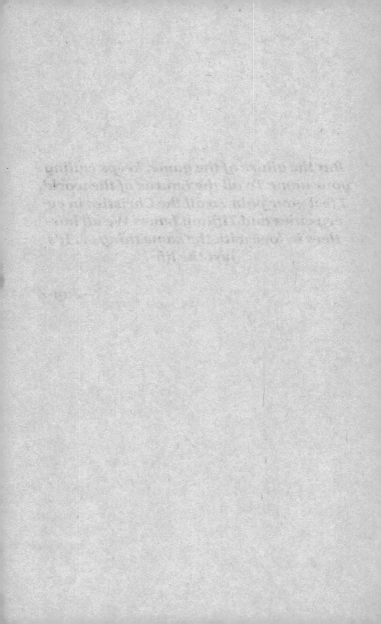

Almost instantly, both of the girls began to yell at each other as they looked at their new boyfriend. Breathing heavily, they both rested about eighty thousand dollars.

Nautica couldn't understand what had happened. Nautica... to each other at Louis Vuitton shook and reasoned. About eighty stacks took it... each dollar band, she pulled no one of the pockets and raised it

BAD BITCHES

Prologue

"Run, bitch! Come on!" Nautica weaved in and out of traffic, trying to avoid getting hit by the cars on the busy Flint street. She gripped the Louis Vuitton bookbag tight and looked back at Khia, who was struggling to keep up in her six-inch stilettos.

Khia quickly snatched off her shoes and ran full speed, catching up with her girl. Both of the girls finally reached Nautica's car and hopped in. Breathing heavily, they both rested their heads on the headrest to catch their breath.

Nautica looked in the rearview to make sure the shooter was nowhere in sight. "We did it!" She double checked her rearview mirrors before opening the bookbag on her lap and pulled out stacks of rubber banded hundred-dollar bills. She was a little shaky from the unexpected shooting, but the money made everything seem a little better.

Almost instantly, both of the girls began to yell in excitement as they looked at their new boyfriend, Benjamin Franklin. About eighty thousand of them.

"Oh my God! I can't believe what just happened." Nautica took a deep breath and stared down at the money. "So this is what eighty stacks look like." A big smile on her face, she picked up one of the G-stacks and kissed it.

"We set, mama. I can't believe—"

Before Khia could complete her sentence, the sound of gunshot blasts and shattering glass rang out. Glass from the back window flew on the girls as the shooter stood twenty feet from them and emptied his clip, bullets flying one after another.

"Go! Go!" Khia yelled as she looked in the rearview and saw the crazed man shooting at them. She couldn't see exactly who he was, but she wasn't trying to stick around and play Columbo either.

I thought the nigga was dead. Nautica scrambled to start the car and threw the shift in drive. As the terrifying sound of bullets thumping the car's exterior serenaded the girls, she sped off, ducking down slightly and peeking over the steering wheel, trying to merge into traffic. The way the bullets were coming, she knew it was an automatic weapon.

Nautica peeked into her rearview mirror again and saw Zion firing his gun. When she finally got far enough distance away for the bullets to stop hitting the car, she sat up and took a deep breath. Her heart beat rapidly, and she could barely drive straight because of her shaky hands.

After Nautica caught her breath, she tried to laugh it off. "Fuck him!" she yelled. "We did it!"

When Khia didn't respond, she looked over at her and saw her staring aimlessly, her head propped against the window. "Khia! Khia!" Nautica yelled. She reached over and shook Khia, and her body fell over, and her head flopped down on the dashboard, revealing a bloody hole in the back.

"No! Nooo!" Nautica yelled. "Don't die on me. We don't die! Khia!"

Nautica kept shaking Khia, but it was no use. The bullet had killed her on contact.

Part One: Trife Life

She looked at the clock and saw that it was
time to get money. She and Rita had been working there together for about two months and had
already figured out a way to embezzle money from
the place.

GOOD GIRLS NEVER TELL

Chapter One

Six Months Earlier

"May I take your order?" Nautica said as she
stuck her head out the drive-thru window at the
run-down chicken spot. She popped her gum and
reluctantly took the customer's order. Nautica ran
her hand through her short, wrapped, black hair,
the hint of cinnamon highlights complementing
her caramel brown skin. Nautica shifted her
weight from one foot to the other for better com-
fort. Although she worked at a food joint, she felt
that heels and perfectly manicured nails were
appropriate. She made six dollars an hour from
Red's Chicken Shack. Well, that's what her paycheck reflected. Actually Red's Chicken Shack
paid her much more than her paycheck read.

She looked at the clock and saw that it was time to get money. She and Khia had been working there together for about two months and had already figured a way to embezzle money from the place.

Khia walked past Nautica and winked as she headed to the manager's office, where TaQuan was. Khia stood about five foot four and was bright yellow with pretty hazel eyes. Though small in stature, Khia was as feisty as they come. She had a beauty mark that rested perfectly above the right side of her lip. Her hair was honey blonde, and her petite figure was just the opposite of Nautica's.

Nautica watched her girl enter the office and close the door behind herself. Nautica knew that was her signal for their lick to go in motion.

TaQuan was a thirty-year-old manager who was slightly overweight and overly gullible. Khia had been flirting with him since she got there, seeing him as a sucker she could get money out of. When Nautica found out that there was no way for him to keep track of the cash count, her hand began to itch; that meant money. His only way to prevent theft was the camera that sat right above the drive-thru cash register. TaQuan would sit in the office all day and watch the girls run the spot while he snacked on chicken throughout the day.

They had a simple plan that worked like gold every time. At a certain time, Khia would go in the office and briefly distract TaQuan so that Nautica could hit the cash register. They didn't get rich off the little scheme, but with that and their nightly stripper job, they got by. They did it at least once every time they worked and split the take at the end of their shift.

Nautica looked at the clock, and as soon as the second hand hit twelve, she took out a couple of twenties from the drawer and stuffed them in her bra.

A few minutes later Khia left the office, a smug smile on her face. She went over to Nautica. "Do you know that fat-ass nigga whipped out his dick?" she whispered, hands on her small hips.

Nautica couldn't help but to burst into laughter. She put her hand over her mouth to muffle her laugh. "Yeah, right, girl. What did you do?"

"What you mean, what I do? I told that nigga he need to step his dick game up and laughed at his ass. That mu'fucka had about three inches at the most. It looked like a li'l Bob Evans breakfast sausage." Khia put up her pinky finger and waved it around. "Did you get the dough?"

"Yeah, I got it." Nautica patted her bra. "I got 'bout three this time."

A car rolled up to the window, interrupting them. Nautica turned around and stuck her head out the window to take the customer's order. She looked right in the face of the infamous Zion Gardin, pushing a cocaine-white Benz with matching leather interior. With the roof completely gone, Nautica got a chance to see the lavish insides. His carpet was even white, obviously custom-made. Just to top it off, his luxury car sat on shiny chrome rims.

Nautica's words got caught in her throat as she looked into Zion's big brown eyes. Naturally, she displayed her pretty smile and tried to say something, but nothing came out. She had heard about him and had seen him in the clubs a few times, but she never could get close to him because he was always in VIP, surrounded by groupies and his entourage.

"Are you going to take my order, ma?" Zion rubbed his neatly trimmed goatee and smiled.

Nautica immediately noticed the guy in his passenger seat. It was bumpy-face Loon, a goon that she went to school with. She remembered how wild and ill-tempered he used to be. She took a quick glance at Loon and then focused her attention right back on Zion.

"Yeah, I got you. Can I take your order?" Nautica asked.

Zion stared into Nautica's eyes. It was an awkward silence. He forgot about the food, and the only thing he wanted was Nautica. Her neatly arched eyebrows, caramel skin, and big brown eyes were many men's weakness.

"What's your name, ma?"

"My name is Nautica. What's yours?" She gently bit the tip of her nail, trying to display her perfectly manicured nails and look cute at the same time.

"You know my name, ma," Zion said arrogantly.

Nautica immediately noticed his swagger and loved his Southern drawl. She wanted to frown at his cockiness, but it only turned her on. He was right. She did know his name, along with every other chick in the city. He was what you called a hood superstar. Every girl wanted to be the chick that rode shotgun with him, because everyone knew he ran the city and pushed heavy coke. That meant he had major paper.

"Yeah, you right. I know your name. Can I take your order, *Zion*?" she asked smiling.

"I want Nautica."

"Sorry, that's not on the menu."

Zion smiled and looked at Loon. He whispered something to him, and Loon immediately hopped in the back seat. "Wanna ride with me?" Zion licked his lips as he looked at Nautica.

Nautica put on a fake frown. "I don't even know you."

"I know, I know. But we got to start somewhere, right? Right now is perfect, feel me?"

"I get off at eleven."

"I can't wait until eleven. Let's ride and get to know each other." Zion put both of his hands together in a praying position. "Pretty please."

Everything inside of Nautica was telling her that she shouldn't do it, but she didn't want to blow the chance of hooking up with a boss. There was a shortage of successful black men in Flint, and she didn't want to miss the opportunity.

Khia nudged her back and whispered, "Girl, go! I will tell TaQuan you got sick or something."

Without even thinking, Nautica snatched off her apron and climbed out the window. Zion helped her jump into his car. Before she even got seated, Zion turned up his music and pulled off.

"Get at me later, fam," Loon said as he jumped out of the car and headed into the Terrace project apartments, one of the seedier areas in Flint, and also Zion's terrain. Nautica was familiar with the area and knew that it was like a city inside a city. Crackheads and heroin users filed in on a daily basis to get their fix from the housing projects. There were strips of apartments all connected to each other, most of which were abandoned. Every sale of heroin, crack cocaine, and weed made inside the projects was a product of Zion's. Zion was what you'd call a jack-of-all-trades, and he had the whole drug game on lock within the projects. The dealers camped out in the abandoned apartments and served the fiends like they were running a drive-thru service. McDonald's didn't have shit on Terrace projects.

Zion hadn't said anything yet to Nautica. He was waiting until he dropped Loon off to officially start their rendezvous.

Nautica was nervous as hell, as she twiddled her thumbs and felt the wind blowing through her hair. Through her rearview, she saw the kids yell and run after Zion's whip, trying to get up close to the spaceship that Zion called his car. A hundred-thousand-dollar car was rare in the hood, and Zion was the closest thing to a celebrity that Flint had seen. Everyone threw their hands up greeting Zion as he rolled by.

I could get used to this shit, straight up! I suppose to be on this nigga arm, Nautica thought as she glanced over at Zion as he gripped the wood-grain steering wheel.

Zion slowly bobbed his head to Jay-Z's "American Gangster," which lightly pumped out the stereo. "So, what you say your name was again?" he asked, his eye on the road.

"Nautica."

"Nautica. I like that name. So, Nautica, why haven't I ever seen you around here? You know. Flint ain't but so big."

"I don't know. I guess you weren't looking hard enough," Nautica joked as she sunk more into the leather seat and got comfortable. Zion had never seen her, but Nautica had definitely seen him. How couldn't she? Every time he entered a room, he was like a magnet for the ladies. He actually had visited the club she stripped at quite frequently, but without her costume and high heels on, Nautica looked very different.

"Guess not." He smiled. "I like yo' style, ma. You are very attractive, and I want you to roll with me today, you know, so we can feel each other out."

"Yeah, that sounds good to me. I want to get to know you too."

"That's cool. But only under one circumstance."

"And what may that be?" Nautica shifted her body to face him.

"You don't repeat or mention anything you hear or see while you with me today." Zion gently tapped his lips with his index finger, as if he was telling her to be quiet.

"Okay. I can keep a secret. Good girls never tell."

Nautica watched in amazement as Zion made runs all over the city. He would just roll up on dudes from different blocks, pick up his money, and toss it in a duffle bag that sat in his backseat; it all seemed so unreal to her. *This nigga is really getting it,* she thought, discreetly checking out the scene. Nautica was definitely impressed by his hustle.

It took him nearly three hours to make all of his runs, and they talked the whole time, about life, the future, politics, and books. Nautica was surprised at how many novels Zion had read. He knew all about street fiction's classic titles and could hold a conversation about any book she brought up. He explained to her that he'd been locked up for two years and reading was all he did then.

They definitely clicked, and Zion was feeling Nautica also. She seemed different than the females he was accustomed to dealing with. Zion smiled as he looked over at her. He could tell that she was impressed, from the slight grin on her face. He knew she thought that he was picking up drug money, but he wasn't; he was picking up extortion money. Zion made different crews around the city pay him on a monthly basis, or he would stick up their corners, making it hell for their operation. When crews tried to jump stupid, he put his murder game down. The town's dopeboys quickly learned that they were better off having Zion as an ally than an enemy.

Zion slyly observed Nautica, and not once did she look at the money when his "workers" paid their taxes, nor did she question him about it. That told him that either she was the daughter of a hustler, or had dealt with one before. She knew the game and how to play it, which, for him, was a plus. That was one less thing he had to school her about.

Once Zion made his last stop, he didn't want the day to end. The sun was setting, and the sun's dim glow reflected off Nautica's skin perfectly. Zion couldn't take his eyes off her and was about to do something he never did. He was going to invite her to his house. Not one of his stash houses, but his home. He had a good vibe about her.

"I don't want to let you go just yet. What would you say if I asked you to come to my house with me?" Zion gently ran his hands through Nautica's hair.

Nautica closed her eyes and enjoyed the feeling of Zion's touch. She took her time before responding. *Well, I don't have to go to the club tonight because it's my day off. Should I go? He seems so perfect. I don't want him to think I'm a ho, though. I'ma go, but he ain't getting the panties. He looks so good, though, he might get the panties. No! No sex, Nautica! No panties!* She looked him in the eyes. "I would love to go, Zion," she said. It almost slipped out of her mouth. She'd agreed to go without even knowing. He had her gone in the head already.

I told myself I wasn't going to do this, but oooh! Nautica gripped the back of Zion's head, guiding him to her favorite spot. She was sprawled out on his king-sized bed, her legs over her head. Zion had gently pushed both of her legs back as far as they could go and teasingly tasted her over and over again. Both of her feet were touching the headboard as she moved her midsection in circles and moaned loudly. Zion took his time rotating his tongue around her spot, and Nautica loved every minute of it. What she thought was going to be just a quick visit turned out to be a sexual escapade.

Zion grabbed a glass of water from his nightstand and took a sip, purposefully leaving an ice cube in his mouth. He went back down on Nautica and applied the cube directly on her clitoris, an O.G. move. It made Nautica go crazy. He treated her lips down below, just as if they were the ones on her face, tongue-kissing them gently and slowly, moaning just barely so she could hear him. He slipped his tongue just a tad bit to her other hole, to let her know that he was a certified freak and knew how to gratify a woman. He slowly rose up and began to pull down his boxers, exposing his rock-hard tool.

Nautica viewed the letters *Z-I-O-N* tattooed across his ripped abdominals. She was so in the zone, she didn't want the feeling to stop, not even for a brief second. She continued to move in circles, and slipped her hand down to her love box, stroking herself slowly, waiting for him. She made eye contact with Zion, and their eyes got stuck on one another, almost like a trance. She usually wouldn't have been so comfortable around a man so quick, but Zion brought the best out of her.

Zion began to put on the condom and watched in anticipation as she masturbated right in front of him. The sight drove him completely insane. Her juices dripped onto his bedspreads, making a small puddle. When he saw her entire pink-ness pulsating, he decided he couldn't wait any longer.

After Zion finished putting on his protection, he then mounted Nautica tenderly. He grabbed his throbbing shaft and slowly inserted himself inside her. She was dripping wet, so he easily slipped in. She was warm inside her womb, and the sensation was the next thing to heaven. He began to slowly thrust in and out, big circles, little circles, up and down, deep and shallow.

Nautica and Zion were in deep unison as they sexed to the Trey Songz playing in the background. Nautica had never had a man take his time like Zion was doing. He went slow but with authority, and Nautica was in total bliss as the name *Zion* rolled off her tongue. Zion whispered things that Nautica never heard and went deeper than any man had ever gone inside her. He was completely turning her out.

Not even ten minutes later, it was over. But it was the best ten minutes Nautica had ever had. She'd had two orgasms and was going on a third when Zion got knocked out the race. They both laid there speechless as they breathed heavily and tried to catch their breaths.

Zion flipped over on his back, and Nautica crawled under his arms and fit perfectly into his body. Zion lightly kissed her on the forehead. He whispered, "This feels right, don't it?"

"Yeah, it does."

Nautica connected with Zion not only on a physical level but mentally also. Although she had only known him for half of a day, she knew that he was going to be her man eventually.

They stayed up until the sun came up, talking about everything, and of course, they had round two. And three.

PLAYIN FOR KEEPS

Chapter Two

"Here he comes," Loon whispered as he gripped his .45 handgun and pressed his back against the wall.

"Shut the fuck up!" Zion whispered back. He pulled the ski mask over his face.

They had been waiting in Mookie's house for over two hours, anticipating his return.

Zion had discovered where Mookie lived a few weeks back and had been plotting on the right time to catch him slipping. This was that moment. He held his double-barrel shotgun and pointed it toward the door as he casually stood in front of Mookie's fluffy sofa.

Mookie walked through the door. He had another man with him. He turned on the light switch and found himself looking down the barrel of a shotgun.

"Welcome home." Zion walked toward the men.

Mookie's henchman didn't even see Loon as he crept up behind him and put a pistol to his neck.

"Fuck!" Mookie put his hands behind his head. He already knew the drill. "You can take off that mask, nigga. It ain't a secret who you are." He kept shaking his head, regretting not being more cautious. He couldn't see himself paying a man to take him off his "to rob" list, but now he was suffering the consequences.

"You right." Zion snatched his mask off and looked into Mookie's eyes.

Zion was known for sticking drug dealers. Zion had the whole city on lock. He only sold drugs in the Terrace projects, but everywhere else was fair game for robbery. Drug dealers actually paid him to not stick them up. He ran with Loon, and everyone knew that Loon didn't have it all and would kill on demand for Zion.

Mookie and Zion stared at each other intensely in a brief moment of silence.

"You playin' fo' keeps, huh, playboy?"

"You know it, baby. But fuck the small talk. Take me to the stash." Zion pressed the barrel to Mookie's chest.

"I don't keep the money here." Mookie shrugged his shoulders. "There's nothing in the house."

Zion smiled and looked at Loon, who had his gun on the other man. Zion gave Loon a nod, and the sound of a .45 blast erupted. Loon shot the man in the back of the head, causing his noodles to fly all in Mookie's face.

"What the fuck!" Mookie yelled in shock as he watched his man fall dead right beside him.

"Don't lie to me, man," Zion said in a calm voice. "We have been tailing you for weeks now. You got two days of your trap in here somewhere. Now I'ma ask you one more time, and if you lie, I'ma let Loon do his thing. Feel me?"

Mookie glanced at Loon, who had an insane glare in his eye, and he knew that look only too well. Loon's trigger finger was itching, and he was ready to pop off. "Damn!" Mookie yelled. He regretted not visiting the safe deposit box that week. "It's underneath my bed in a safe."

Zion laughed and nodded at Loon again.

Loon aimed his gun at Mookie's leg and let off another round, instantly dropping him to his knees.

Zion bent to one knee, so he would be face to face with the whimpering Mookie, who was gripping his wounded leg. "Why are you playing with your life, son? We already checked in that safe under yo' bed. That's where you keep this, right?" Zion pulled out a black 9 mm from his back pocket. "What you thought? We were rookies? You watch too many movies, nigga. You thought you were going to go to the box and start blasting, huh? That ain't how shit go in real life. I'ma ask you one more time—Where's the dough?"

"Man, it's in the freezer in the basement."

"In the freezer? I would have never thought of that." Zion smiled, knowing that he was about to hit a lick. He quickly rushed down the stairs and headed for the deep freezer.

Once Zion was in the basement, he cracked open the freezer, moved around some of the frozen vegetables, and just as Mookie promised, there were Ziploc bags with neatly stacked hundred-dollar bills in them. He rubbed his hands together. "That's what I'm talking about!"

Zion quickly ran back upstairs to grab a garbage bag and tell Loon that the money was where Mookie said it would be. He nodded at Loon, signaling to him that the money was downstairs, and almost instantly, Loon put a bullet in the back of Mookie's head, rocking him to sleep permanently.

Mookie grunted just before he fell face down on the carpet, where a small puddle of blood began to spread, turning the beige carpet maroon. The air quickly began to stink of human waste. Mookie had eased his bowels on himself, because of his relaxed muscles.

Loon smiled as he stared at the body. The stink had become so familiar, it didn't even bother him anymore. He stepped over Mookie's dead body, like it was litter on a city street, and followed Zion down the stairs, where they both began to pull the money out of the freezer like madmen and tossed it into a heavy-duty garbage bag.

Nautica, wearing a thong-and-bra set and a gold see-through wrap tied around her waist, oiled her butt cheeks in circular motions as she looked at her profile in the full-length mirror. The bass from the speakers on the main stage shook the floor in the back dressing room, where the scent of musk mixed in with various female body odors drifted around the room. She shook her head. She hated the fact that she degraded herself for money, but she did her best with the hand she was dealt. "I got to get out this mu'fuckin' strip club, straight up!" she mumbled to herself as she pulled her garter belt up to her thigh. She'd been working in Magic City for six months and always told herself that she would make five thousand dollars and quit, but that day was yet to come.

Her mind began to drift as she thought about Zion and the incredible night they'd shared the night before. She smiled as she thought about their bonding so quickly and naturally. She felt her love button pulsate just at the thought. She also had flashbacks about the way he put it down in the bed. And she loved that they talked for hours after they'd had sex, great sex at that, and it was never a dull moment. Nautica didn't know if it was because she hadn't had sex in a while, or because he had the stroke of a genius. Either way, she loved it. *I can't believe I slept with him on the first night, though.* Something overcame her the night before, and she found herself being more freaky than ever.

Nautica was definitely planning on seeing Zion again. In fact, they'd made plans to have breakfast the next day. Mentioning that she was a stripper always worried her when she talked to a guy, and with Zion it was no different. *I'll wait until he gets to know me,* she thought. Her eyes shot to the dressing room entrance when she heard the distinctive loud voice of her cousin Khia coming from the main floor and into the dressing room.

Khia wore a full-body fishnet suit that hugged her body tight and left nothing to the imagination, which was just the way she liked it, raw and uncensored. She sashayed in slowly in her six-inch stilettos, shifting her hips as she walked, making her plump ass cheeks sway back and forth. On the small of her back, a tattooed *Q* inside a black rose displayed her loyalty to her man, Quaye.

"Hey, girl, you up next!"

Nautica looked at Khia and instantly knew that she was "rolling"—a term Khia used to describe being high on ecstasy pills. "I know. I'm on my way out right now," Nautica said as she hurried out to make her grand entrance.

"Oh, yeah! Fellas, I got something fo' y'all tonight. Coming to the stage, put yo' hands together for Naughty!" the DJ yelled into the microphone as the sounds of Young Jeezy began to rock the house.

Zion and Loon walked into the club iced-out, both of them wearing all black and shades. Zion slipped the bouncer at the door two hundred dollars to let them slide in with their guns, always a necessity for their line of work. They bounced their head to the rhythm of the music as they made their way to the back of the club to get a table. Zion usually sat in the VIP section, but on that night he wanted to just relax and not draw attention to himself. They maneuvered through the crowd and found a seat at a back table. Zion waved over a waitress just before he sat down.

"Yo, life is good right now," Zion said, nodding his head to the music.

"That's for damn sure." Loon thought about the twenty-eight grand they'd just taken from Mookie.

As they got settled in, Zion took a closer look at the stripper on the stage that swung on the pole. Normally he wouldn't remember a face, but the performance that she'd put on the night before had her etched into his mind. It was Nautica. Zion smiled as he watched her do her thing, bouncing her assets on stage like a seasoned veteran.

Loon noticed that Zion's eyes was stuck on the dancer. "Yo, ain't that shorty you scooped up yesterday?"

Zion answered, "Yeah. I didn't know she was a stripper though."

When the waitress came over, Zion ordered a bottle of Rémy Martin and two shot glasses. He then slipped her a hundred-dollar bill to tell Nautica to come see him when her performance was over. Zion licked his lips and rubbed his hands together, knowing that it was a must to see Nautica again. The day before, he'd made it appear to her that he was a hustler, but that wasn't how he got down. Only a select few knew he was a thief, but he knew that profession was less appealing to the women, so he let Nautica come up with her own assumptions.

Nautica finished off her set with a grand finale by slowly sliding down the pole and landing in a split and making her butt cheeks jump up and down, one then the other. The crown erupted with cheer as she got up and began to pick up the dollar bills scattered all over the stage. Nautica hurried off stage as she stuffed the crumbled bills into her bra. She wiped the sweat from her forehead and chest, as she made her way to the back room to freshen up before she walked the floor for lap dances.

Just as she stepped off stage, Angie came over to her. She said excitedly, "Yo, you have a request in the corner." She threw her head in the direction of Zion. "He's spending big money too!"

Nautica looked over and squinted her eyes to get a better view, and after a brief second of staring she noticed him. *Damn, what the hell! I didn't want the nigga to find out like this. Fuck it, he was eventually going to discover it anyway.* She walked to the back to freshen up, switching hard just in case he was looking.

Ten minutes later Nautica strutted out of the back wearing a different two-piece than she had on before. She headed over to Zion's table, where she saw Loon and him taking shots. "Hey, Zion," she said smiling as she stood before him.

"Hey, *Naughty*," he said sarcastically. He smiled at her and scooted over in the booth, so she could have a seat next to him.

"Shut up." Nautica playfully hit him. "This isn't how I wanted to tell you about my night job, but I guess it's not secret now, huh?"

"Nah, but it's cool though, ma. I see you about your paper. I understand." Zion poured himself another shot and looked at Nautica's body up and down. "I had a great time with you, though. Shit was crazy, right?"

"Yeah, I have never been like that before. Something came over me."

Zion smiled but remained silent. He knew why she was so "sexually free" on that night. He had slipped some ecstasy into her drink and gave her a little help with her confidence by doing so. It was something that Zion did often to females just to ensure that he would have fun. "So what up, ma? When can I see you again?"

"I get off in a couple of hours . . . if you want to wait."

"Sound like a plan," Zion said, hoping he had more ecstasy pills left in the car.

Next Morning

Nautica walked into her apartment that she shared with Khia. She was trying to shake the headache that she had from the night before. She and Zion had been up all night sexing, rolling on ecstasy pills. When Zion first showed her the pills, she refused, but he was very persuasive and got her to pop one. After she experienced the way it made her feel, she popped them all night without a care in the world. She dropped her gym bag at the door and plopped on the couch. The smell of bacon and eggs filled the air, and she heard someone in the kitchen moving around.

Moments later Khia joined her in the living room and sat on the couch next to her. "I thought I heard you come in." Khia began to eat her breakfast. "How did it go?"

"It was okay. We stayed up all night rolling. He did his thing last night," Nautica said, referring to Zion's sex game. She got up and walked into the kitchen to grab a fork.

"I can tell he did. You walking like you got a stick up yo' butt."

Nautica yelled, "I did have one up there!" and disappeared into the kitchen.

Both girls burst into laughter.

When Nautica returned, she sat on the couch next to Khia and began to eat breakfast off her plate.

Khia got up to turn on the television. "So, you feeling that nigga Zion, huh?"

"Yeah, he's cool."

"I heard he getting that paper too. That's always a plus."

"You got that right. Shit, I'm trying to come up." Nautica looked around the small two-bedroom apartment.

"Oh yeah, I wanted to talk to you about something," Khia said as she sat back on the sofa, "but you left the club so quick."

"Okay. What's up?"

"Well, you know how I've been going up to Saginaw to buy my knockoff purses?"

"Yeah." Nautica stuffed her mouth with the wheat toast.

"Well, while I was up there, I met a nigga name Roland, and he a ol' trickin' nigga. I met him while at the mall, and on spot, he offered to buy all my purses."

"Yeah?" Nautica said, her interest piqued.

"No joke. I let the nigga take me out to lunch, and he a clown-ass nigga. He kept talking about how much money he had and kept flashing knots of money. He took me back to his spot, a nice house out in the suburbs. After a couple drinks, he showed me about twenty-five thousand dollars in shoeboxes, trying to stunt. You know what light bulb went off when I saw that, right?"

"I already know what you thinking." Nautica smiled. "You set it up already?"

"You already know."

Khia danced seductively in her birthday suit and red pumps and sucked her breast as Roland sat in his La-Z-Boy and watched. Nautica was standing behind him and giving him a massage. Roland couldn't believe he had stumbled upon a freak like Khia. She had set up a meeting at his house, telling him she was going to bring a surprise. He'd never thought that the surprise would be another woman.

About six foot tall and medium-built, Roland had a bald, shiny head and looked about thirty years old. In all of his years, he never experienced anything so erotic. His tool began to grow as he felt Nautica's tongue on the back of his neck.

"Yeah, baby. That feels good." Roland closed his eyes and gripped his pipe through his jeans.

Nautica raised his arms as she slid off his shirt, displaying his flabby-looking upper half. *Nigga need to do some pushups.* She tossed his shirt.

Khia continued to dance around the spacious, plush living room, shaking her ass in a slow, wavy motion. Then she got on her knees and crawled over to Roland and placed her head in his crotch. She began to unbuckle his belt with her teeth, exposing his small, hard penis that barely stuck out the hole in his boxers. She pulled off his pants and began to kiss around his midsection.

Nautica put her hand over her mouth, trying not to burst out laughing at his tiny tool. Khia shot Nautica a look, and Nautica knew they were thinking the same thing.

Khia tried to not giggle. "Oh, you so big," she said in a seductive voice.

Nautica grabbed Roland's arms and placed them behind the chair, and he smiled as he looked down at his erect pencil and waited for Khia to take him into her mouth. Just as he was about to instruct Khia to give him head, he felt the cold steel of handcuffs lock both of his hands behind the chair.

"Oh, hell yeah," he said, his fantasies coming true.

Khia pulled out two pairs of her own handcuffs from her handbag and shackled each one of his legs to the base of the chair. At that moment the massaging hands stopped from Nautica, and Khia instantly stood up.

"What's up? Why y'all stop?" Roland opened his eyes, and a little drool rested on his lips.

"Nigga, please! Where the dough?" Khia went over to grab her jeans and put them on.

Nautica began to put her clothes on also.

"What the fuck are you talking about?" Roland didn't fully realize that he'd just got tricked. He tried to release himself from the heavy chair, but it was useless.

"Nigga, stop being stupid. Where the cash at? Under your bed?" Khia pulled a gun from her handbag, a gun that her boyfriend Quaye had left at her house to do the caper.

Roland continued to try to free himself. "You dirty-ass bitch!"

Khia walked over to him and hit him with the butt of the gun, causing him and the chair to fall over.

"Yeah, yeah. But where the money?"

Nautica began to empty all the china cabinets, looking for a jackpot.

"Nautica, here." Khia gave Nautica the gun and headed to the back room to look under his bed. "Watch this nigga. I'ma about to go to the shoeboxes."

Nautica sat on the couch and looked at Roland, who lay on the floor, bound to the chair.

"Man, you don't have to do this," he said in a desperate plea to Nautica.

Nautica couldn't help but laugh as she looked at his awkward position and his little man that stuck out of his boxers. She sat back and closed her legs as she enjoyed the hilarious scene. "Nigga, shut up," she said in between laughs.

"Look, come on, this ain't even my house!" he said as he tried to position himself upright. "Just let me go, and I won't hurt you, okay."

Nautica got tired of all the small talk and walked over to him. She grabbed one of his balled-up socks and shoved it deep into his mouth, shutting him up. "That's much better." She smiled.

Khia came out of the back with two shoeboxes. "Come on, I got it," she said as she walked over to her and grabbed the gun. "This nigga still lives with his momma!" Khia looked at Roland with disgust.

"How you know?" Nautica asked.

"The other room had pictures of an old lady, and it smell like Bengay in there. This ol' frontin'-ass nigga still lives with his damn momma." Khia shook her head from side to side. "All the damn bills are in a Betty Dixon name. This nigga was straight flaking. That's yo' momma's name, ain't it?" Khia looked at Roland and laughed at the way Nautica stuffed his mouth.

Just then, the girls heard the door being unlocked. They froze as their eyes shot to the front door. Khia pointed the gun toward the door, waiting to see who was coming in.

An elderly lady came in, followed by two more ladies around her age, with bingo markers in their hand. Khia quickly put her gun behind her back and smiled.

Betty jumped, startled by her houseguests. "Oh my God!" She put her hand on her chest. "Roland, I told you not be having these fast-ass girls in my house. You got some ol' freaky stuff going on, don't you?" She put her hands on her hips and began fussing.

Nautica and Khia smiled and walked past the ladies and headed toward the door. Nautica looked back at a squirming Roland, whose muffled screams echoed through the house. "Sorry, miss, we just got a little carried away. Your son is a little on the freaky side."

"I know, with his nasty ass. I should leave his ass lying on the floor just like that. Got yo' shit all out in front of my friends."

Betty's bingo friends smirked as they looked at Roland on the ground, his business peeking out of the hole in his boxers.

Nautica and Khia left for Flint with two shoeboxes full of cash. Enough to hold them off until the next caper.

SPACESHIP

Chapter Three

Nautica and Khia strutted down the long hallways of the Genesee Valley Mall. They both had on big designer shades and thigh-high boots that fit snug over their tight blue jeans. Khia wore her long hair down freely, while Nautica had her hair pulled back tightly displaying her soft baby hair that rested on her edges.

It was three weeks since they'd robbed Roland, and after they paid rent and went shopping a couple times, they were broke again. They had spent a full day of shopping together, and both of their hands were full of bags, courtesy of TaQuan's credit card.

Nautica and Khia bought some food from Burger Joint and sat down at the food court and placed their bags at their feet. "How did you get the nigga to give you his card, Khia?"

"What do you mean, bitch? I let him taste the kitty cat!" Khia snapped her fingers.

Both of the girls burst into laughter.

"So you and that nigga Zion serious, huh?"

"No, it's not like that. I only been fucking with him for a couple of weeks. Why you ask?"

"Just seem like y'all tight, that's all. I haven't been seeing a lot of you lately."

"I know yo' ass. What do you have up yo' sleeve?" Nautica squinted her eyes, trying to read her cousin. "When you get to asking questions, you usually have something up."

"I'm just saying—"

"You saying what?"

"I know Zion is getting money. Shit, everybody know he getting it. Maybe we can hit his ass," Khia said nonchalantly. She put a fry into her mouth.

"I don't know about this one, *K.* I haven't even got a chance to peep him out yet. And, anyway, you know the rules—no in-town licks," Nautica said, reminding Khia of their rule to never rob a hustler in the same city as them.

"Yeah, I know, but I just had to throw it out there. Times are rough out here. Shit, I got bills to pay."

"Bitch, me too. But we can't do something that's going to come back and bite us in the ass later."

Khia nodded in agreement and dismissed the notion. Khia was what you call an opportunist and always looked at a baller as a potential victim.

Although Nautica declined the offer, Khia had planted a seed that would stay in the back of her mind. She changed the subject before Khia got any more ideas. "Remember how we used to always talk about moving to New York and becoming big movie stars?"

"Yeah, I remember. Girl, we always said we were going to buy matching drop-top Benzes and shut down the Apple."

"We can still do it. We just got to get out this ghost town-ass city." Nautica sipped on her Coke. "Sometimes I wish I could get on a spaceship and just fly away from this mu'fucka."

"That sounds like a plan, girl. Let's make a pinky swear that we're going to leave this city and hit the Big Apple and show them New Yorkers how real bitches do it." Khia playfully held up her pinky and reached over the table.

Nautica smiled and locked pinkies with her cousin. Although they were being playful about it, they both were dead serious.

Nautica walked around in Zion's place wearing a red lingerie set that she knew Zion would love. The velvet two-piece hugged her body tight as she walked around and lit the candles that she'd strategically placed around the bedroom. She had been dating Zion for nearly a month and a half and wanted to do something special for him. She had just popped an ecstasy pill and was preparing to give him the time of his life.

Zion had given her a key to his place just a week before, and she put it to good use that day. She'd called him and told him that she would meet him at his house in about an hour, which gave her plenty of time to set up the bedroom. Her plan was to wait in the closet for him, and when he entered the room, she would come out and blow his mind. She glanced at the clock and smiled, knowing that he would be walking in any minute.

Just as she was about to turn on some slow jams, she heard keys jingling. She quickly grabbed the bottle of wine off the coffee table and hurried into the bedroom closet and hid. She could see the whole room through the shutters in the blinds. She held her breath, bottle of wine in hand, and heard him come into the room. But Nautica noticed it wasn't her man in the room. It was Loon. He went straight to Zion's safe and began to put in the combination.

Nautica didn't want to hop out the closet and expose her half-naked self to Zion's flunky. *What the fuck is this nigga doing here? He has a key too?*

As Loon began to put the money into the safe, a phone rang.

"Hello," Loon said. "Yeah, I'm dropping it off right now. No, nobody is here. She didn't make it here yet, I guess. Cool. Bye." He flipped down his phone and emptied the rest of the bag.

That must have been Zion. Nautica wished that Loon would hurry up and leave. Loon began to exit the room, but then he stopped just before reaching the door and walked back toward Zion's dresser.

"What is this nigga doing?"

Loon looked around, probably to convince himself that the coast was clear, then reached into Zion's top drawer, the place where Nautica kept her underwear whenever she overnighted at his place. Nautica's eyes got big as golf balls when Loon took a pair of her underwear out and began to sniff them. He had an insane look in his eyes as he lay on the bed and pulled out his penis, all the while sniffing Nautica's panties.

"What the fuck!" Nautica witnessed Loon masturbate right on her man's bed. *This nigga is nasty.* She turned her head away in disgust when she saw the look on his pale, freckly face.

Seconds later, Loon released himself into Nautica's panties and stuck them back into the drawer. He then got up and quickly left the room.

When she heard the front door slam, she came from out of the closet. "Oh my God, this nasty mu'fucka is foul as hell," she yelled, ripping the blanket and sheets from the bed. She had to stop herself from gagging as she dumped all the clothing from the top drawer into a garbage bag. "Wait until I tell Zion," Nautica said to herself. "He is gonna nut the fuck up!" She threw the blanket into the washing machine.

Nautica finally understood now why Loon never said anything to her. He had a fetish for her. She picked up the phone to call Zion but stopped when she thought about how much Loon meant to him. Zion would always tell her that Loon had it hard growing up and was a troubled soul. Instead, knowing Zion had a bad temper, she decided to just keep her distance from Loon's deranged ass. She shook her head as she made her way to the living room. Loon had completely ruined her sexual appetite. *Loon doesn't have it all.* She knew he was a little bit off, but she'd never expected anything like she'd just witnessed.

TIME CHANGES EVERYTHING

Chapter Four

"Fuck that!" Zion yelled. He sat on the sofa counting money that he'd just robbed from a hustler in Detroit. "You ain't going to no strip club. I don't care who birthday it is!"

"But, baby," Nautica pleaded, "it's not going to be like that. It's just a little private party to celebrate Khia's birthday." She stood in front of him with her arms crossed, trying to sway his decision.

Zion shot a cold stare at Nautica, and if looks could kill, she would have been in a body bag.

Nautica took a deep breath and stormed into the back room. She slammed the door and flopped down on the bed. She looked around the plush room and realized that it wasn't worth being imprisoned. She had been with Zion for three months, and it didn't take long for his true colors to come out. She found out that he was possessive and controlling. *This nigga tripping. He doesn't want me to go anywhere!* Nautica folded her arms across her chest and sat there sulking.

Meanwhile Loon sat in Zion's kitchen counting up money and remained silent as he listened in on the conversation. Nautica never said anything to Loon after what she'd seen him doing with her underwear a while back and acted as if he didn't exist when he was around. She always grew an uncomfortable feeling in Loon's presence.

Zion looked over at Loon and signaled for him to leave, so that he could talk to Nautica alone, and almost instantly, Loon stopped counting the money and exited the house. Zion focused his attention back on Nautica. He shook his head from side to side, not seeing why she would want to be in a strip club again.

Although Zion gave Nautica any and everything she wanted, he took her life away from her, and began to exhibit his jealousy more and more each day. Zion had her trapped and made her quit the strip club and cashier job, telling her, "My woman don't work." But that only made her dependent on him, which was just the way he liked it.

It didn't take long for her to realize how he got down. He would come in at night with blood on his clothes and duffle bags full of bloody money, and it scared her to death. One night she even walked in on him and Loon counting up a table full of money, ski masks pulled to the top of their heads. She always wondered when karma would get Zion, and would she suffer for his wrongdoings. She would have never dealt with him if she knew the truth, because she knew what came with being a stickup kid.

Zion came in the room and saw Nautica on the bed moping. He stood in front of her and ran his fingers through her hair, trying to change her mood. "Baby, brighten up." He took a seat next to her.

Nautica remained silent and kept her act up, hoping to change his mind.

Zion rubbed her back. "You know how much I love you, right? I just want you to get away from that life. That strip club is your past, and I don't want you in that type of environment."

"But it ain't even like that. Khia's birthday is today, and I told her I'd be there."

Zion stood quickly and raised his voice, "Fuck that! You can go to the mu'fuckin' club, but after that you find you another place to live! Ain't no woman of mine going to be in a nasty-ass strip club. Birthday party or not, I ain't feeling the shit!" Zion said, getting more angry with each word. He had offered Nautica a place to live, so she and Khia wouldn't be cramped up in the small apartment they'd been sharing. And once he found out that Khia's boyfriend spent the night there from time to time, he wasn't having it. He insisted that she move in with him and he would take care of her financially.

"Zion, I don't want to leave here. I love you. I just thought that it wouldn't be a big deal." Nautica's eyes began to water.

Zion calmed himself and gently grabbed her face. "I tell you what, I will pay for a shopping spree for you today, okay. You will be so busy looking at all the things you bought, you won't even be thinking about a birthday party." Zion knew how to get Nautica to see things his way. "And I have something else that will cheer you up." He pulled a Tylenol bottle out of his pocket.

Nautica's eyes lit up. She already knew what it was. A new batch of ecstasy pills. She had developed the habit of rolling and loved the way sex felt while on the drug. Zion loved the way it felt too.

She quickly snatched the pills out of his hands and jumped off the bed. Then she popped open the bottle and put a pill in her mouth before scooting back to the bed.

Zion smiled as he dropped his pants. He was about to have Nautica just the way her loved her. High.

Loon sat in his small apartment in the Terrace Projects looking through the blinds of his front window at the crack-heads and nightwalkers walking up and down the block. He gripped his .45-pistol and clenched his teeth, paranoia driving him crazy. He'd done so much mischief with Zion, thoughts of retaliation from his robberies and murders bombarded his mind. He shifted his eyes nervously, as he took deep, slow breaths. He suffered from paranoia and anxiety every night, and this was a normal routine. Most nights he fell asleep by the window, two guns in his hands. Zion had manipulated his mind and turned him into a coldblooded killer with no sense of remorse.

Loon, aka Fremont Williams, had met Zion in the Terrace projects when he was twelve years old. He often wished he could go back to that time. A time when he was innocent. When he had a soul. A single tear slid down his cheek as he thought about all the murders he had committed over the years. He wiped the tear away and chuckled to himself, trying to shake the sadness off.

Loon had had a rough childhood. He lived with his father Gene, an ex-con, who was forced into single parenthood when Loon's mother died suddenly. On his eleventh birthday Loon found his mother dead on the bathroom floor. She had gotten a bad pack of dope and died shortly after injecting the drug. That's when he met his father, who'd just been released from prison.

Since Loon's mother didn't have any family, the court looked to his father's side and appointed Loon to live with his grandmother, but at her old age, there was no way she could keep up with him, so Loon did most of his living with Gene.

It wasn't long before Gene began to display his homosexual tendencies, which he'd developed while incarcerated. At first he would just make Loon bathe and dress in front of him, but as time passed, things got progressively worse, and no matter how much he tried not to look at his own son in a sexual way, his sexual appetite got the best of him. Not only that, Gene also developed a bad heroin addiction.

Loon thought back to the time when he was first given his nickname "Loon."

Six Years Earlier

"Come on up in here, Fremont," Gene called after he finished up the smack that he'd copped from one of the corner boys. He wanted to get a blowjob from his son before he slipped into one of his nods. Gene was sick and twisted in the mind and felt that what he was doing wasn't wrong.

Fremont reluctantly inched into the room and stood before his father. Fearing that Gene might strike him for not moving fast enough, Loon's small frame tensed up.

Gene slowly pulled out his manhood and began to stroke himself. "Come on, Freemont! Do what yo' daddy like, okay." He scooted down in his La-Z-Boy and threw his head back.

Tears slid down Loon's cheek as he dropped to his knees and began to do the most horrific act that any young boy could experience.

Hours later, Gene was finally out of his nod. The combination of the good smack and an orgasm had him in a deep sleep for two hours. Once he woke, he yelled, "Freemont!" He wiped the drool from his mouth and reached into his pants to search for his last twenty-dollar bill.

Freemont, eyes bloodshot from all of the crying he'd been doing, walked into the room and stood in the doorway.

Gene waved the twenty-dollar bill in the air. "Go and cop yo' old man a 'doo,'" he said, meaning a twenty-dollar fix. Gene owed so many dope dealers money, he didn't want to risk running into one. So, to be on the safe side, he always sent Loon out to the sharks for his medicine.

Loon took the twenty-dollar bill from his father and hit the streets with what seemed like the world's weight on his shoulders. "I swear, when I get older, I'ma kill that fool!" he said to himself as he stormed down the block in search of a corner boy.

Loon looked down at his worn-out clothing and shoes and began to shake his head in embarrassment. He never had up-to-date gear or shoes, and got teased and talked about in school because of it. All of the teasing and name-calling pushed him to be a withdrawn child, so he barely even spoke. That's why the kids in school gave him the name Loon, saying he was loony, and a nutcase.

Loon finally reached a group of young boys sitting on a stoop. He approached them, his head down, and threw up one finger, which meant he wanted one pack.

A couple of the boys in the group who went to school with him and ragged on him on a daily basis wanted to mess with him again. One of them said, "How you gon' be on dope in middle school?" Then he laughed and slapped five with some of the others. The boy reached into his pocket and pulled out a doo. "Yo," he said, a mischievous smile on his face, "give me the money first."

Now the golden rule of the streets was, the product and money was supposed to be exchanged at the same time, so when the boy suggested that Loon give him the money first, the other boys already knew what was about to go down.

Loon gave the boy the money, and the boy snatched it and stuffed it into his pocket. "Thanks, homey," he said, and everybody burst into laughter.

Loon said in a low voice, "Can I please just have the doo?" He kept his head down, avoiding eye contact with any of the goons.

"Get the fuck out of here, nigga!" The boy pushed Loon to the ground.

Loon slowly stood back up. "Man, please just give me the money or the doo." He had tears in his eyes now, more so from embarrassment than pain. Loon saw that the boys were having too much fun antagonizing him, so he turned around and headed home to "hell's kitchen." He cried a river on his way back, as he thought about the repercussions of returning empty-handed.

Hours later, Loon sat balled-up in a corner of the house sobbing hysterically with a black eye and a sore body. His father was upset at him for not bringing him back his dope, and showed Loon no mercy, beating him for almost an hour. At first Gene only used a belt, but the more he thought about missing his high, the more he used his fist on his son.

Loon flinched at the sound of the front door slamming. He knew that his father had left out for the night, as he did many nights when he didn't have his fix. Loon thought about getting revenge on the corner boy who'd caused him so much pain. *All he had to do was give me the doo*.

He stood up and began to pace the room. Without even thinking, he went to his father's room. There, he lifted up the mattress and pulled out a rusty old pistol. He gripped the metal and examined it like it was a rare work of art. A twisted smile formed on his face, even as the tears continued to flow. This was only the beginning of Loon's madness.

The flames from a burning apartment building illuminated the projects, and the air was smoke-filled. A group of boys watched the fire like it was a Fourth of July spectacle.

Zion pressed his back against the wall and pulled the ski mask over his face. He'd been watching the corner boys make crack sales for the past hour and was waiting for the perfect time to stick them up. He was glad for the fire, because it temporarily got the corner boys off their square, which made his job a little bit easier. He gripped the .380 handgun, switched off the safety button, and slowly sidestepped toward the edge, preparing to give them a big surprise.

Just as Zion was about to rob them, he saw a young boy walk briskly past him and toward the crowd of hustlers, so he fell back.

It all happened so fast, he was caught off guard. Two gunshots rang out, and the sound of the boys scattering and scrambling for their life filled the air.

Zion peeked around the corner and saw a young boy with a smoking gun standing over a body. Zion couldn't believe his eyes. The boy didn't look a day over twelve.

The boy turned his head and saw Zion looking on in astonishment.

Zion studied the boy's face and noticed the blank expression.

The boy then looked back at the dead body and he went into the boy's pocket. He pulled at a wad of money, peeled off a twenty-dollar bill, and threw the rest of the money on top of the dead boy's body. The boy then broke down and dropped to his knees. He dropped the gun and covered his face with both of his hands and started to cry.

Zion rushed over to the boy and placed his hand on his head. "Yo, you gotta get out of here before the police come, young'un." He grabbed the wad of money off the boy and rushed over to the tin coffee can where the corner boys kept their drugs at. "Bingo," he whispered to himself when he found a couple ounces of crack cocaine and bundles of heroin within the can. He looked back at the boy and noticed that he hadn't moved an inch. Zion said with more urgency this time, "Yo, son, you gotta go before the police come."

The young boy still didn't move. He just stared at the fire blazing from his own home

Zion followed the young boy's eyes and wondered why he took so much interest in the fire when he had just killed a person. Zion did a double-take and looked at the young boy closer. *That's faggot-ass Gene's son.* Zion's older brother and Gene did time together. Zion's brother had told him that Gene was a butt-buster in prison, and when he was released acted as if he wasn't a homosexual.

Loon had shot his father and set the house on fire. Then he came out to shoot the boy that stole from him. From that day, Zion took him under his wing and molded him into a ruthless killer.

Zion and Nautica lay in the bed completely naked and breathing heavily. They'd just finished up a nice sex session. Feeling dizzy, she rested her head on Zion's chest.

He began to stroke her hair and admire her smooth caramel body. "Nautica, sorry for getting so angry earlier, but you know I'm crazy over you. I just don't want you to get into your old lifestyle at the club and all. You are so above that shit, babygirl. I just want the best for you," he said, never taking his eyes off her behind.

"It wasn't even going to be anything like that. I just wanted to show up and tell her happy birthday, like I promised her I would."

"Well, check this out. I gotta go to Detroit to handle some business tonight, but while I'm gone, you can go shopping. I'll leave you some money on the kitchen counter. That way tonight you will be so busy looking at the stuff you bought, you won't even be thinking about a birthday party." Zion tried to bribe her into staying. He knew that Khia would have niggas crawling out of that club and wanted Nautica as far away from that scene as possible. His jealous streak a mile long. He hated for Nautica to be in the company of men without him being there.

Nautica thought it best not to argue, especially since Zion was sponsoring a shopping trip. "Why do you have to go to Detroit tonight? Aren't

you leaving for Baltimore in a couple of days? I
wanted to chill with you before you left."

Zion frowned up. "What the fuck you mean?
How you know I was going to B-more this week?
I never told you that."

Nautica wanted to take her words back. She
knew she'd said too much. She took a deep breath.
"Well, since we've been kicking it, you always
leave on the fifteenth of every month for a couple
of days. You always come back with receipts from
B-more, so I put one and two together." Then
she changed the subject." So, you're leaving me
tonight, Zion? I get worried about you when you
take your trips. You always come back with blood
on your shoes and bags full of money. The money's good, but . . . I don't want you to lose your life
for the love of the money. I know you rob people,
Zion. You have more guns than socks." She playfully pinched him.

"Yeah, Nautica, I hear you, but I have to go.
I have to handle this business, all right." Zion
and Loon had planned on robbing a Detroit
hustler later that night. They had been on him
for months and finally got the information they
needed to hit him.

"Okay," Nautica whispered in a disappointed
tone. "Thank you for the shopping trip."

Nautica thought about what she would wear
to Khia's party. She knew that handling business

meant that he'd be out late. She had planned to just show her face at the party anyway and slip back home before Zion realized she was gone.

She looked up at Zion and gave him a kiss. Nautica rubbed his chest and felt the ecstasy drug kicking back in as her love button began to pulsate once again. She slid her hand down to her love button and began to touch herself.

Zion sat up and watched Nautica please herself. He thought it was a good time to ask her about his fantasy. "Baby," he whispered in a low, husky tone, his member growing.

"Yes, daddy," Nautica said, her eyes closed and her legs wide open.

Zion reached to her breasts and fondled them. "What would you say if I wanted a threesome?"

Nautica paused and gave him an are-you-out-yourdamn-mind look, but the sensation of her erect clitoris clouded her thoughts.

When Zion realized she wasn't going for it, he decided to not ruin the mood. He slid down and got in between her legs, in a position where his face was eye level with her pussy, and went to work. Zion knew that she would eventually come around to it, if he got her high enough, so his plan was to be patient and wait for the right time to convince her to see things his way.

BIRTHDAY JUMP-OFF

Chapter Five

It was the just after 11 p.m. when the owner of Magic City closed the strip club for the night so Khia could have her birthday bash. The club was semi-full, since and it was more of a personal party for Khia. She felt funny being fully clothed at Magic City, a place where she'd usually be half-naked in high heels.

Everyone seemed to be having a good time, and the DJ played Sade, giving the club a different feel than its usual. Khia looked around for Nautica. She'd been seeing less and less of her cousin ever since she'd started dealing with Zion. *Where is this girl at? She swore she was coming.* Khia looked at her watch.

Khia happened to glance at the door, and in came Nautica with her long mink on, commanding attention from everyone in the room, her shiny diamond earrings blinging every time the light hit them right.

"Hey, girl!" Khia yelled as she ran up to Nautica with open arms.

Nautica smiled and rushed to the birthday girl. "Happy birthday, *K*!" She hugged her cousin tight and rocked back and forth.

"I'm glad you came. Now it's time for this party to pop off!" Khia reached over into the bucket of ice and grabbed a bottle of Moët.

Nautica, scared of what might happen to her if Zion found out she snuck out to the party against his wishes, walked to the back of the club with Khia. She didn't want him to put her out on her behind. Though Nautica was a hustler's hustler, her instincts to fend for herself and get money had partially fallen off since she'd been with Zion. She'd become so comfortable with him giving her money, she didn't have any money saved up to fall back on.

Nautica and Khia sat down at the back table. The party was getting interesting, and had a good vibe, as people took to the dance floor, but Nautica had a slight headache from the ecstasy pills she'd taken earlier, one of its side effects, and had planned on staying just for an hour or so, to show her face, and then return home. *He's going to Detroit tonight anyway,* she thought. *He won't get back until at least four in the morning.*

"So how's everything going with you and Zion?"

"I can't complain. He treats me good and gets me whatever I want," Nautica said without enthusiasm. "What more can I ask for?" She'd been with Zion for the past three months and gradually began to find out how possessive he was. She didn't want to talk about him anymore, because it only reminded her of how much she was beginning to not like him.

"Shit ain't the same at Red's without you. You know ol' girl that worked at the front cash register?" Khia asked, referring to the girl they had worked with at Red's Chicken Shack.

Nautica nodded. "Yeah. That pale chick, right?"

"Yeah, that dumb bitch. Do you know I tried to put her on the lick we used to do, but that bitch couldn't get it right. TaQuan caught her ass redhanded stuffing that shit in her bra. The bitch was too slow. You know how we used to do."

"Fifteen seconds and out," they both said in unison as they slapped each other's hands and burst into laughter. They both had been schemers since they were young and they knew each other like the back of their own hands. They hustled niggas, jobs, and whatever could be hustled together. It was evident that they were two peas in a pod.

"Damn, I miss you, girl," Khia said as she looked at her best friend and cousin.

"I miss you too girl." Nautica saw that Khia was getting misty-eyed, so she shifted the conversation. "Where is my nigga, Quaye?" Nautica asked as she took off her coat.

"Oh, he's up there in the DJ booth." Khia pointed to the corner of the room.

Nautica looked over and saw Quaye talking to the DJ.

Moments later Musiq Soulchild's "Teach Me" filled the airwaves, and Khia immediately closed her eyes, put her hands up, and began snapping to the rhythm, swaying back and forth. "Girl, you know this my song." She stood up.

Nautica and Khia watched as Quaye made it over to them. Quaye smiled when he saw Nautica and kissed her on the check. "Hey, sis!" He always called her his sister. They weren't real siblings, though, but had been tight since high school. Actually Nautica was the one that hooked him up with Khia.

"Hey, big bro!" Nautica said as she hugged him.

Quaye looked over at Khia and smiled. He looked at her with pure admiration and was deeply in love. He extended his hands so that he could dance with her. "Come on, baby," he said, giving her bedroom eyes. "This is your song." He had requested that particular song for Khia.

"Quaye, these heels are killing me. Nautica, take this dance for me." Khia nudged her cousin. Nautica was the only girl she would let Quaye dance with without feeling any jealousy.

Nautica laughed and stood up. "Come on, bro. Don't be stepping on my toes and shit. You know yo' ass got two left feet." Nautica followed him to the dance floor.

Khia watched on as they headed to the dance floor and began to dance. Moments later, while Khia was taking swigs of her Moët, she saw Zion and Loon enter the club. From the look on Zion's face, she knew that he was heated. Zion's eyes scanned the room, like an eagle looking for his prey. She rushed over to the front, trying to block Zion's path. "Hey, Zion! Nau—"

Zion brushed her off and went straight past her when he spotted Nautica snapping her fingers in the air, and slow-grinding with Quaye. He couldn't bear the sight. "Move, bitch!" he mumbled, headed to an unsuspecting Nautica, whose back was turned to him.

Zion had changed his mind about the caper that he had planned for the night and turned around and went home. When he didn't see

Nautica, he immediately knew where she had crept off to.

I told her ass not to come to this mu'fuckin' club with that ho. Zion approached Nautica, with Loon close behind. He reached for Nautica's hair and yanked her back and whispered in her ear through clenched teeth, "What the fuck are you doing here dancing with this nigga? Huh?"

"Zion, stop. You're hurting me!" Nautica tried to grabbed his hand and pull it away from her hair.

Khia rushed over and started screaming at Zion. "Let her go, nigga! Why you comin' in here and actin' a damn fool?"

"Shut up, bitch!" Zion never even looked at Khia.

Quaye instantly got offended and ran up on Zion, but before he could even do anything, Loon had a pistol pointed to his forehead. The DJ instantly cut the music, and all you heard was chatter throughout the club, as all eyes were on their fiasco.

"Easy, my nigga," Loon said calmly as he coldly stared at Quaye.

The club turned into complete pandemonium. People began to scatter, trying to pile out the club's single exit.

In the midst of all the chaos, Zion still had Nautica's hair wrapped around his fist. "I told yo' ass that I didn't want you down here, didn't I?" he said, his grip getting tighter by the second.

Before Nautica could even respond, she found herself on the floor.

Khia was yelling obscenities, but all of her rants fell on deaf ears. Zion picked Nautica off the floor and practically pulled her out of the club.

Loon struck Quaye with the butt of his gun and watched as he fell to the ground in pain. He pointed the gun at Quaye's head and smiled as he saw the fear in Quaye's eyes.

"Loon, let's go!" Zion yelled as he pulled Nautica toward the exit. He glanced back at Loon who stood over the man, pointing his gun. "Let's go," he yelled again as he briefly stopped. He then felt Nautica trying to pull away from him. "Where the fuck you think you going?" He wrapped his hand around her neck and squeezed.

"Zi—Zion, I can't breathe." Nautica tried her best to get him to unleash his grasp, but he was much too powerful for her.

Khia jumped on Zion's back and began beating him upside his head. "Get off her, you bitch-ass nigga!" she yelled as she delivered another blow to Zion's head.

Zion, without taking his hand from around Nautica's neck, flung Khia clear across the room, crashing her into some tables.

Quaye quickly scrambled to her side, but was helpless, because he wasn't strapped.

Zion pulled Nautica out and pushed her in the backseat of his truck that was parked in front of the club. He slid in next to her and remained silent. Soon after Loon jumped in with them and drove off.

"What the fuck is your problem!" Nautica yelled as she began to cry. She smacked Zion across the face.

Zion shot a look at her, and just the look alone scared the shit out of Nautica. She scooted away from him and held her hand up, just in case Zion was going to strike her. Zion looked at her and shook his head from side to side.

Nautica continued to cry. *I'm done with this crazy nigga. It is over!*

Zion watched Nautica as she slept peacefully in his bed. He looked at the box with the Tiffany's necklace that he held in his hand, his peace offering for the way he acted the night before. The sight of Nautica grinding against another man sent him over the edge. He bent over, trying to wake her with soft kisses. "Wake up, Nautica," he whispered in her ear. He placed the pink box next to her face. Once he saw Nautica open her eyes, he left the room.

Nautica flinched out of fear, seeing Zion over her. She quickly sat up and picked up the box on the bed next to her and opened it. The diamond hoop earrings blinged as they sat propped up inside the box. Although Nautica loved the earrings, she hated who they came from. She heard Zion leave the house. *This nigga thinks he can buy me something and I will forget the bullshit he pulled last night? He's gotta be out of his mu'fuckin' mind.*

A feeling of queasiness overcame Nautica, and she suddenly had the urge to vomit. She got off the bed and rushed to the bathroom. She reached the toilet just in time to release herself, vomiting profusely.

After two minutes of hovering over the toilet and gagging, she fell to the floor, lightly sweating. She took a couple of deep breaths before she stood back to her feet. "What the fuck is wrong with me?" she whispered as she braced the sink with both hands.

Tears streamed down Nautica's face as she rode on the passenger side of Khia's car. So many thoughts crossed her mind. She had just left the doctor's office, where she found out she was three weeks pregnant. She placed her hand on her stomach, thinking about the life currently growing inside of her.

Khia maneuvered the Lexus that Quaye had just purchased her. "Whose is it?"

"What the fuck you mean? It's Zion's crazy ass. I can't believe this shit, girl." Nautica was going crazy with the thought of bringing a child into the world with Zion as a father. "I can't keep this baby, Khia. I'm not even feeling Zion like that. Especially not enough to be having the nigga's baby. I don't know what to do."

Khia reached over and placed her hand on Nautica's lap.

"It's going to be okay, girl. But I think you really need to think about this before you do something you regret later." She glanced over at her cousin and saw the pain and disappointment in her face.

Nautica weighed the good and the bad about having a baby, and no matter how she thought about it, the outcome was a negative one. She knew that Zion was leaving for Baltimore in two days, which would give her time alone to make one of the hardest decisions in her entire life— whether to keep the baby or not. In the meantime, she would keep the news of her pregnancy away from him.

BALTIMORE LOVE THING

Chapter Six

Two Days Later

Nautica and Zion pulled into a suburban area just outside the city of Baltimore. Nautica was half-'sleep as she leaned far back in her seat with her feet propped up on the dash. She felt Zion's hand rest on her inner thigh.

"Wake up, baby. We here." Zion pulled into a five-star hotel that sat next to an extravagant upper-class shopping mall.

Nautica sat her seat up and began to rub her neck and yawned. She still felt the pain from the fight they'd had a couple of days earlier. Zion leaned over and gently kissed Nautica on the cheek. She slightly turned her cheek and smiled on the outside, but she was burning up on the inside. *This nigga always trying to act like shit all good after he pull some foul shit.* She crossed her arms and remained silent. Zion had begged her to take the trip with him. He thought he could amend things on his trip to Baltimore. It wasn't working, though, because Nautica had said barely anything to him the whole eight-hour drive there.

Nautica got out of the truck and followed Zion as he entered the revolving-door entrance to the hotel. The sound of Nautica's stilettos clicked on the marble floor as they made their way to the front desk to check in.

Zion wrapped his arm around Nautica's waist and kissed her on the neck. "I got a surprise for you when we get upstairs," Zion said as he took the room key from the desk clerk and made their way to the elevator that led to the room.

Zion was rubbing his dick and Nautica's ass the whole way to the room. Nautica knew what his surprise was and wasn't exactly excited about what was about to go down. As soon as they entered the room, he pounced on her. Nautica couldn't even put down her bags good before he was kissing on her neck.

"Slow down, Zion. Damn!" Nautica said as he roughly handled her. She knew she couldn't have sex because of the abortion she'd just undergone. She'd decided that bringing a child into the world wasn't good for her right now. She couldn't stand Zion and couldn't see dealing with him for the next eighteen years. She wanted to give him oral sex before he tried to go all the way, but knew that it would be difficult, especially if he was on ecstasy.

"Come on! Shit, I'm hard as hell right now." Zion ripped her blouse open, exposing her breasts. The only thing on his mind was getting inside of Nautica. He had business to handle in an hour, so he wanted to get off before he left.

Nautica instantly dropped to her knees and began to unbutton his pants. She prayed to God that Zion didn't pull down her pants, because she still had on the oversized pad that she got from the abortion clinic. *I hope this nigga ain't trying to fuck. What am I going to tell him? He knows I get my period at the beginning of the month and it's the middle of May. Fuck! I betta give him the best head ever, so he won't want any sex.*

Nautica wrapped her lips around Zion's thick pole. He was telling the truth, because he was hard as a rock. She did her best Superhead impersonation, grabbing Zion's pipe with both of her hands, twisting and massaging it, while she sucked on it. Zion grabbed the back of her head and began to force himself deep inside her mouth. Nautica wanted to gag so badly, but she knew she couldn't break his concentration, which could have ruined the mood and give him a chance to ask for sex.

I hate him. He was never this rough in the beginning. Nautica moaned while hitting him off. "Uhmm!" She knew he was about to explode, the way he was pumping.

Not even a second later, on cue, Zion came in her mouth. He threw his head back in pleasure and grabbed the back of Nautica's head and forced all of himself down her throat.

She immediately jerked her head back and spit his semen out. "What the fuck!" Nautica yelled as she wiped her face.

Zion knew that Nautica hated when he did that. He couldn't help but smirk at the sight of her spitting his juices out. He quickly wiped the smile off when he remembered how violent he'd been with her the day before. He knew that he had to act extra nice to her for the next couple days to get back in her good graces.

Zion picked up his Louis Vuitton bookbag that he put the re-up money in. He had them in neat stacks, each rubber band containing five thousand dollars. He pulled out a stack and tossed it to Nautica.

"Okay, baby, this is for you. I have to go handle some business in the city, but there is a big mall next door. You can go there and pick you up some things while I'm gone." Zion said nonchalantly.

"Thanks, Zion," Nautica whispered without enthusiasm. She flipped through the hundred-dollar bills.

Zion stuffed the bag back under the bed and got completely naked. He walked into the bathroom to take a shower, so he could get ready to meet his connect.

Nautica sat up on the bed and held her stomach tightly. She began to think about the abortion. *I should have kept my baby. No, fuck that! If I had his baby, he would really think he owned me then.*

Nautica kept replaying the scene at the club in her head. Zion had never put his hands on her, and that took her completely off guard. From that day she knew they could never be.

She stood up and began to pace the room, talking to herself quietly, of course, so Zion wouldn't overhear her. "That mu'fucka got to be out of his damn mind. I'm no man's property! After this trip, I'm quitting his crazy ass."

Nautica stopped at the bed where Zion put the money, and a wave of nosiness came over her. She listened close, to make sure the shower was still running. She grabbed the bag and cracked it open. Her eyes lit up when she saw stacks and stacks of money. She knew he was getting money, but she didn't know it was like that.

Everything in her heart told her to take the money and make a run for it, but she knew Zion would come after her. That's when she decided that she would rob him. Just not at that moment. She would kill him softly and rob him without him knowing it was her.

Nautica's oversized Dior shades covered her eyes, and the sound of her stilettos echoed through the mall as she turned every straight man's head when she walked by in her hip-hugging Rocawear jeans, and Chanel scarf stylishly draped around her neck. *Yeah, I'm a bad bitch.* She smiled to herself.

As she entered Bloomingdale's, she felt her phone vibrating in her purse. She looked at her caller ID. It was Khia. "What's up, K?"

"Hey, girl. You okay? That nigga was foul as hell the other night," Khia said. The last time she'd seen Nautica, she was too distraught for her to bring the fight up, but now, days removed from it, she wanted to know what went on.

"I know. That's exactly why I'm about to quit his ass. He crazy as hell." Nautica said as she picked up a blouse.

"Ain't he? What happened after you two left the club?"

"He got to apologizing and shit, talking about, he doesn't act like that all the time. I don't have time for his shit."

"I feel you, girl. Leave that clown-ass nigga alone. But, anyways, where you at? I stopped by your house earlier."

"Oh yeah, I came out to B-more with the nigga. He was all in my face, and trying to be all lovey-dovey and shit. The only reason I came out here is so I could use his ass and make him take me shopping."

"I heard that! Did you tell him about the baby?"

"It's no baby to tell him about, Khia. I got rid of it." Khia didn't know what to say, so she just left it alone.

"What's in Baltimore, anyway?"

Nautica looked around to make sure no one was by her to overhear her conversation. "He came out here to cop from his connect."

"Word? He let you roll with him?"

"Yeah, and the nigga brought so much dough up here with him. The nigga getting it! I got something for his ass, though."

Nautica was already putting a plan down in her mind. She was going to make him pay for putting his hands on her. She finished up her conversation with Khia and continued shopping.

While shopping, Nautica noticed a man staring at her from afar. She looked him up and down. He definitely wasn't her type. He was dressed nice, but his shaped-up curly 'fro and little shades weren't up to par. *Look at this square-ass nigga.* She rolled her eyes and turned her back on him. She sifted through the designer blouses and held one up to her body to see the look. Before she knew it, the man had approached her, his shades propped on top of his head.

"Excuse me, miss," he said in a kind tone.

Nautica, without even looking at the man, acknowledged him, "Yeah?"

"I don't mean to bother you, but I noticed your beauty and your style when you were walking through the mall and—"

"Look, brotherman, I'm not trying to be mean or nothing, but you ain't my type." She cocked her hip to the side and rested her hand on it.

The man took a step back and chuckled. "Look, ma, it ain't that type of party," he said with a heavy Baltimore accent. "Honestly, you're not my type either. Especially with you wearing that Chanel scarf with a Louis Vuitton purse." He looked her up and down and flashed his iced-out Rolex watch.

Nautica instantly grew embarrassed, knowing that she wasn't on her shit that day, wearing Chanel and Louis together.

"I approached you because I am a casting director for *The Wire,* and I was wondering if you did any acting."

"Oh, I'm so sorry, but you know how guys are sometimes."

"I understand. But you have a unique look and you're just what I'm looking for, for a particular small role." He looked her up and down once again, not the way other men looked at her, but in a talent-scout way.

"Well, I'm not from here," Nautica said, not fully believing the man. "I'm just here on vacation."

"Well, let me give you my card, and if you come back to town, give me a call." He pulled out a business card and handed it to Nautica.

Nautica looked at it. The card had his name, Benny Donovan, and his office and cell number. She couldn't believe she was getting approached by a casting director. A big smile spread on her face. When she looked up, he was already walking away. Nautica glanced at the card again just before slipping it in her purse. "*The Wire*, huh?" she said to herself.

"That's the spot right there. Nigga, you better not bust yet! Keep hitting that spot, daddy," Khia moaned as she gripped the kitchen seat tightly. She had nothing on but her high heels and a smile.

Quaye had his pants dropped around his ankles, one foot out, and his Timberland boots on as he grinded slowly in circles, trying to hit every wall inside of Khia. His balls swung back and forth with every stroke, hitting Khia's clitoris every time, and it was driving her crazy.

"I got you, ma."

Quaye gripped Khia's gigantic butt cheeks and massaged them as he went to work on her. His sweat, along with Khia's juices hit the ceramic floor, and the sounds of sex echoed throughout the kitchen. Quaye had a habit of keeping his boots on when he had sexual intercourse with Khia. He knew that it would provide more grip, and that meant better sex for both of them.

Khia felt Quaye's warm manhood pulsate so hard inside of her, it felt like his soldier had its own heartbeat. "Oh my goodness!" She gripped the sink even tighter as he gave her the business. She began to play with herself, feeling her orgasm about to approach.

Quaye knew what was coming, so he sped up, and the sound alone drove both of them crazy.

Khia's knees buckled as she climaxed and exploded, staining Quaye's Timberland. She almost lost her balance and held the sink to keep herself up as her legs quivered uncontrollably.

Quaye pulled out in time to release himself on Khia's lower back.

"I love you, boy," Khia said out of breath, hovering over the sink.

"I love you too, baby. I'm sorry, but I had to handle that. It's something about seeing a woman in the kitchen that makes me go crazy."

"No apologies needed. You handled yours today." Khia put her hand up for a high-five.

Khia made her way to the bathroom to take a shower. She thought about how she was going to tell Quaye he was going to be a father, something she'd found out earlier that morning. She didn't know how he would take it.

She hadn't even told Nautica yet. It was ironic that they were pregnant at the same time. She wished that Nautica had kept her child so that their children could've grown up together, like they did.

As Khia got in the shower and let the water cascade down her body, she smiled. She was fond of the idea of being a mother-to-be. That was the only way she'd slow down and get her life together. This was her ticket to change her life around and get out of that strip club.

She couldn't wait to call Nautica to tell her, but then she thought about what had happened a couple of nights before and began to worry about her. *That nigga Zion is nuts. Nautica better quit that nigga, fo' real*, she thought as she continued to wash her body.

Zion drove back from meeting his connect, which was about an hour from the hotel he was staying at. He had twenty bricks of cocaine stuffed in hidden compartments in his bumper and in a dummy gas tank under the car. He was going to make it snow in Flint. He had a plug from his old cellmate on some unstepped-on cocaine out of B-more and took advantage of it. He went back and forth from B-more to Flint at least twice a month. Loon usually rode with him, but he made an exception this time, since he wanted to make Nautica feel good after he'd fucked her up.

Zion bobbed his head to Rick Ross and felt his phone vibrate on his hip. "Yo," he answered.

"What's good, family?" Loon said.

"Ain't nothing. Got them thangs on deck though. It's fishscale too," Zion said, referring to the bricks of cocaine he'd just copped. Most hustlers called pure cocaine *fishscale* because of the shiny flakes in the powder that resembled the scales of a fish.

"Word?"

"Yes, indeed. Yo, did you take care of that business for me?"

"No doubt. I took care of that this morning. Caught the nigga at the crib slipping. He was all laid up with a little broad. He didn't even see the shit coming. I hit him while shorty was in the shower."

"Good job, young'un. You hit the bitch too, right?"

"Naw, didn't have to. I went the ski mask way. And, plus, she was in the shower and didn't hear a thing. I was in and out. Feel me?"

"You know I taught you better than that, young'un. No witnesses. If you going to half-step, you in the wrong business. Shoulda hit her too, Loon. But, anyway, I will be home tomorrow evening. We will talk then. One."

"A'ight. One."

Zion smiled, knowing that Quaye was forever 'sleep. He hated that Quaye pushed up on his woman, so he had his killer take care of that problem immediately. Quaye's death would be like a trophy for him to show the hood—Don't fuck with Zion's property. Even though Quaye was dead, the thought of him coming at Nautica still got him angry.

Nautica hauled all of the bags from her mini-shopping spree into the room and noticed that Zion hadn't made it back yet. She took a deep breath and dropped the bags on the floor. She flopped down on the bed, her mind racing. The only thing she could think about was all of the money she'd seen in Zion's bag earlier that day. She'd created so many different scenarios in her head to rob him, and none of them seemed flawless.

I should just have a nigga run up in his shit. I know exactly where he keeps his money at his house. Naw, I can't do that. He keeps that crazy-ass Loon with him twenty-four seven. That nigga is like his personal watchdog. I'ma have to come up with something. Whatever she did, she knew she had to do it soon because she wasn't going to stay around much longer.

Nautica felt her stomach begin to turn flips and she cringed at the pain. The doctor had told her to expect bad cramps after the abortion, and that's exactly what happened. "God, it hurts," she murmured as she curled up into a fetal position and wrapped both of her arms around her stomach. Just then she heard Zion open the door.

Zion was still upset from thinking about how friendly Nautica was with Quaye and wanted to make her feel some pain. He'd planned on having anal sex with her for the first time, to get her back for grinding on the guy from the club.

Nautica quickly sat up and tried to hide the pain. "Hey, baby."

Jealous thoughts on his mind, he said nothing as he dropped his pants and walked toward her.

I just took care of him earlier. Nautica quickly got tense and nervous. Not knowing what to do, she said the first thing that came to her mind. "I can't, baby. I came on earlier today."

Zion knew that Nautica had an abortion earlier that week. He thought she was cheating, so he had Loon follow her. When Loon broke the news that she went to the abortion clinic on Flushing Road, Zion was furious. He didn't know if Nautica was pregnant by another man or if she just didn't want to have his shorty. Either way, he hated her for it. The thought of his seed being killed intentionally was against all of his beliefs, and from that point, he decided that Nautica would be nothing more than a jump-off to him.

"You don't come on until the beginning of the month," he said as he tried to unbutton her pants. "Stop playing."

Nautica squirmed away and moved his hands. "Baby, I'm serious. My cycle has been all mixed up lately since I've been taking birth control," she said, hoping he would buy the story.

Zion frowned. "What the fuck you mean, birth control?"

"I went to the doctor last month to get some. You know how you don't like to use condoms, Zion. I am not trying to have a baby right now." Nautica crossed her arms and hugged her midsection tight.

Zion had been intentionally trying to get her pregnant the past three months, so that he could put handcuffs on her. *So that's why she hasn't gotten pregnant until just now. She must've forgotten to take them when her ass got knocked up. I thought my shit wasn't working or something. Grimy-ass ho!* He looked at Nautica in disgust. "A little blood won't hurt. If I'd walk through mud, I'll fuck through blood." He dropped his boxers, exposing his erection.

Nautica didn't want to refuse him. He had the same look in his eyes that he had at the club when he choked her. So she just lay there while he had his twisted way with her. Tears slid down her cheek as he went in and out of her. At that moment, Nautica decided to set Zion up. *This is the last time he's going to hurt me,* she thought as tears continued to flow.

"Nooo! Oh my God! Quaye!" Khia screamed as she cradled Quaye in her arms. Blood leaked from his head and was all over the place. He stared into space, barely breathing. "Baby, no!" she yelled, looking into his eyes.

After getting out of the shower, she'd found him in their bed shot, and immediately called 9-1-1 to their home.

Khia's breaths became shallow. She gripped Quaye, knowing that things didn't look too good. "Come on, baby, just hang on for a minute until the ambulance gets here," she said, trying to sound as calm as she could.

As the blood from the gunshot wound continued to flow onto her and the floor, Quaye twitched. He looked into Khia's eyes, knowing that he was about to leave the earth.

She took his hand and placed it on her stomach. "You're going to be a daddy. You can't die," she whimpered, wiping the sweat from his forehead.

Quaye tried to fix his mouth to smile, but the pain was much too much to bear. He glanced down at her stomach and then back into her eyes. "I . . . I love you," he said in a whisper. Then he gave up the fight.

"Nooo!" Khia yelled, Quaye's dead body in her arms.

MÉNAGE À TROIS

Chapter Seven

One Month Later

Nautica sat in the vanity mirror in her room and slowly stroked her hair. She was nervous as hell as she looked down at the "special k" pills, a nickname for the drug ketamine, which causes blackouts and temporary comas. Doctors use ketamine for patients undergoing surgery. She and Khia had been putting a plan together, and Khia had gotten the pill from a friend that worked at a pharmacy. The pill resembled ecstasy and would be great for the job.

Nautica had told Zion she was down for a ménage à trois. And he was game. She had convinced him to let her go with him on the trip once again, telling him that it made sense to leave for Baltimore from the hotel room the morning after the ménage. He always left Flint at or around 6:00 A.M., to make it to Baltimore by the afternoon, so Nautica knew he would have the money already bagged up and ready to go to, as he always did before every trip.

Nautica was waiting for Khia to call her so they could go over the caper one last time before they made it to the hotel room. She began to wonder if Khia was mentally ready to go through with the escapade. Ever since Quaye's funeral, she'd been acting differently, and only opened up to her when they were discussing robbing Zion. But, besides that, she'd also become anti-social.

The phone buzzed, startling Nautica. It was Khia. *I can't believe I'm about to do this.* She reached for it. Just before she picked it up, she saw Zion appear in the doorway. "Zion! You scared me," she said, pushing the ignore button on her phone.

Zion had been looking forward to this event all week. He always wanted to have sex with Khia, so for Nautica to propose a ménage à trois with her was a dream come true. "Don't be scared, ma." He walked toward her and stood directly behind her. He looked at her through the mirror. "I'm glad you came around. Tonight is going to be fun. You just gotta relax." He began to give her a light massage.

Nautica hated the feel of his cold touch and couldn't wait to kiss Zion and the city goodbye for good.

Zion could feel the tension in her shoulders and knew exactly what would loosen her up. He reached into his pockets and pulled out a Tylenol bottle almost full with ecstasy pills.

Nautica saw the bottle and knew that it was a no-no for her to be rolling that night. She had to stay on point and focused for what was about to go down. "No, let's wait, Zion. And, plus, Khia has some good shit from Detroit. She said it's better than the bullshit we have around here." She glanced up at him. She could tell by his eyes that he had already started rolling.

"Whatever floats yo' boat," he said just before stuffing the bottle back in his jeans.

Nautica looked at the time on her phone. *An hour and a half until it goes down.* She stood up and faced Zion. She looked down and saw that he was partially aroused. She sexily licked her lips and dropped to her knees.

Zion smiled as and began to unbuckle his pants. The ecstasy had him hot and ready. He watched Nautica search for his pipe and pull it out of the hole in the front of his boxers. She slowly began to tongue-kiss his tip and play with his balls, and he threw his head back in complete bliss. Within seconds he was rock-hard and ready to dive into something wet.

Nautica put her mouth on his manhood and took all of him inside her mouth and then quickly pulled back. She stood up and began to walk out of the room, leaving him with a stiff one.

"Hold on, ma. What you doing?" he said in an almost begging tone.

"The party doesn't start until Khia gets here. I have to go get dressed at her house, and we will meet you at the room, daddy." Then she grabbed her car keys from the nightstand and disappeared into the dark hallway.

Nautica picked up Khia, and they were on their way to the hotel. "Girl, I'm nervous as hell," she whispered as she drove. She glanced over at Khia, who had a stone-cold mug on her face. Nautica saw Khia's eyes begin to water and she began to think about backing out.

Khia wiped her eyes and smiled. "I'm nervous too, but we know what we have to do. This will solve all of our problems. We will never have to scheme and hustle for money again. We could move to New York, like we always talked about, and pursue a modeling career. Don't bitch up now, Nautica," Khia said, getting louder and louder.

Just then they arrived at the Radisson Hotel. Nautica turned into the driveway and turned off the ignition.

Khia noticed Nautica's facial expression. "Stop being so damn scared!" She pulled down the visor mirror so she could touch up her makeup.

"Chill the fuck out! I just want to think about this before we do it. I mean, Zion is crazy as hell. What happens if he finds us? Then what? You didn't think about that shit, did you? He would kill both of us!" Nautica shouted.

An uncomfortable silence filled the car as both girls thought about what had just been said between the both of them. The clock on the car's CD player showed it was ten o'clock, the exact time they were supposed to meet Zion at the room.

Nautica began to think about Zion's bad treatment, and though she hated to admit it, she had a bad ecstasy problem, which Zion introduced her to. "Let's do it." She nodded her head up and down.

"That's what I'm talking about!" Khia leaned over and kissed Nautica on the cheek.

"Ughh, bitch, don't kiss me." Nautica playfully wiped the kiss away.

"Okay, you got the pills, right?"

"Yeah, I got 'em." Nautica reached into her trench coat pocket and grabbed the aluminum foil the pills were in. "We need to do this quick and get the fuck out of there. As soon as he nods off, we get the money and leave this ghost town for good."

"Cool with me. I already kissed Mama goodbye and told her we were leaving for a while." Khia rubbed her hands together, thinking about starting a new life with the money. "How much did you say he usually takes to re-up?"

"Eighty thousand, I think."

"Cool. Yo, park on the street." Khia pointed to the curb.

"Why not pull up to the room door?"

"So no one sees us leaving."

Khia and Nautica walked up to the door and knocked. After a few seconds of no response, Nautica noticed that the door was cracked and ready for their entrance. They walked in and closed the door behind them. Nautica locked it after she closed it. J.Holiday played lightly in the candlelit room, and the flickering light provided just enough glow for their shadows to grace the wall.

The girls saw the silhouette of Zion's body sitting in a chair in the corner. He had already begun to provide the spacious room with the aroma of Kush weed and had a bottle of Hennessy on the table next to him.

After walking in slowly and seductively in identical long trench coats and six-inch heels, swaying their hips back and forth in unison, like they were marching to the same drum, without saying a word, they both climbed on all fours at opposite ends of the bed and stared at each other with bedroom eyes, just like they had practiced. Zion was in complete ecstasy as he watched his personal show.

Nautica and Khia both slid off their jackets, exposing their already oiled naked bodies. Zion smiled as he admired the beautiful bodies in the king-sized bed. The two girls' bodies were so different, but equally sexy. Nautica had a plump, caramel behind, with small breasts and weight in all the right places. On the other hand, Khia had a high-yellow tone and big, perky breasts on her petite body. Her behind wasn't as plump as Nautica's, but it was small and firm. Her nipples were pink and big, while Nautica had small dark circles around her pointy nipples. Khia's light skin complemented Nautica's brown complexion, creating a perfect blend. *Mocha and crème*, Zion thought as he unzipped his pants and let his tool escape his jeans.

Pumps still on, the girls moved smoothly to the music as they positioned themselves for a sixty-nine experience. They acted as if Zion wasn't in the room and buried their faces in each other's crotch without licking, moving their midsection to the same rhythm. They were giving Zion an illusion, and the slurping sounds they made misled him into thinking they were going for it.

Zion couldn't take any more. He downed the double shot of Henny he had in his cup and put out the blunt that hung from his mouth, without taking his eyes off the girls. He stood up, completely erect and equipped to join their session. He walked to the bed and stood over them, trying to think of a way to join in without disrupting the flow.

When Nautica noticed Zion in her peripheral view, she gently pinched Khia's inner thigh, letting her know it was time for the second step of their plan.

Khia got off Nautica and began kissing Zion and rubbing his nipples, distracting him so Nautica could get the pills out of her coat.

Nautica eased off the bed and got the pills from her pocket. She then walked over to the table and grabbed the bottle of Hennessy. She took a deep breath and glanced over at the side of the stand, where Zion's Louis Vuitton bag sat—the same one he always carried his money in. *Hell yeah,* she thought as she watched Zion passionately kiss Khia and rub the tips of his fingers on her love button.

She crept up behind Zion, who was still standing, and began licking his muscular back. Nautica sat the special k pills on her tongue. Then she grabbed Zion's jaw and turned his face toward her to kiss him and, in the process, slipped the pills in his mouth. She then gave him the Hennessy bottle. "Here, baby, wash it down with this," she said in her most seductive voice.

Khia lowered herself and took Zion into her mouth.

"Oooh, shit!" Zion grabbed the bottle from Nautica and took a swallow to wash the pills down.

Nautica then climbed on the bed and began to masturbate while Zion was getting head from Khia. Zion was turned out. He felt like he was having an ongoing orgasm. He stared at Nautica's fat, juicy lips that sat between her legs as he grabbed the back of Khia's head and stroked her mouth like it was a vagina.

Come on, mu'fucka, fall out! Khia pretended she was enjoying what she was doing.

Nautica wondered how long it'd take for the drug to kick in. *Pass out, nigga.* From what Khia had told her, it took place immediately, but Zion was showing no signs of dizziness or confusion. She wondered if the drug was going to work. She then got on all fours and began helping Khia with the blowjob. Zion threw his head back, his eyes closed and a smile on his face.

Khia let Nautica finish the blowjob as she slipped off the bed and reached for her purse.

While Nautica continued to satisfy Zion, she felt his legs get wobbly. *It's kicking in.*

Without warning, a loud sound erupted, knocking Zion back. Khia had just sent a bullet through his chest.

Nautica screamed in shock when she saw Zion topple over the table and fall to the ground. She looked back at Khia, who possessed a look of hatred in her eyes as she held the smoking gun. Nautica reached over and snatched the gun from Khia. "What the fuck are you doing, K?" Nautica yelled, her hand shaking nervously with the gun.

Khia was still staring at Zion with her lips tight, and pure hatred in her heart. She knew Zion had ordered her baby father's murder, and she finally got her revenge.

"Oh, shit!" Loon whispered. He almost dropped the video camera. He was taping through the shutters in the closet, something Zion had asked him to do. This wasn't their first time doing this either. *What the . . .* Loon's eyes grew big as golf balls. He regretted leaving his gun in his car as he looked at Zion breathing heavily and holding his chest. *Dirty bitch.* His adrenaline was pumping now as he watched Zion fight for his life, blood pouring from his torso. He wanted to bust out of the closet to help his mentor, but he knew that would be suicidal. It took all of Loon's self-control for him not to jump out of the closet. He still had the camera rolling as he watched the two girls and listened closely.

Nautica yelled, "What the fuck are you doing?" She stared at Khia like she was crazy.

Khia walked over to Zion and spat on him. "This bitch-ass nigga had Quaye killed. I know it was him," she said, tears streaming down her face. "Quaye didn't hurt anybody. He didn't have not one enemy ever, and all of a sudden, after that stunt at Magic City, he got killed. He killed my Quaye! So now he is about to die! He killed the father of my baby!"

Nautica cocked her head to the side and frowned. *What baby?* "Bitch, are you crazy? You wasn't supposed to kill him. And where in the hell did you get that gun?" Nautica watched Zion gasp for air.

Khia then snatched the gun from her and let off another round in Zion's body.

Nautica sat there in shock as she stared at the dead body. She quickly snapped out of her daze, put on her coat, and grabbed Zion's Louis Vuitton bag. "Come on! Let's get the fuck out of here."

"Run, bitch! Come on!" Nautica weaved in and out of traffic, trying to avoid getting hit by the cars on the busy Flint street. She gripped the Louis Vuitton bookbag tight and looked back at Khia, who was struggling to keep up in her six-inch stilettos.

Khia quickly snatched off her shoes and ran full speed, catching up with her girl. Both of the girls finally reached Nautica's car and hopped in. Breathing heavily, they both rested their heads on the headrest to catch their breath.

Nautica looked in the rearview to make sure the shooter was nowhere in sight. "We did it!" She double checked her rearview mirrors before opening the bookbag on her lap and pulled out stacks of rubber banded hundred-dollar bills. She was a little shaky from the unexpected shooting, but the money made everything seem a little better.

Almost instantly, both of the girls began to yell in excitement as they looked at their new boyfriend, Benjamin Franklin. About eighty thousand of them.

"Oh my God! I can't believe what just happened." Nautica took a deep breath and stared down at the money. "So this is what eighty stacks look like." A big smile on her face, she picked up one of the G-stacks and kissed it.

"We set, mama. I can't believe—"

Before Khia could complete her sentence, the sound of gunshot blasts and shattering glass rang out. Glass from the back window flew on the girls as the shooter stood twenty feet from them and emptied his clip, bullets flying one after another.

"Go! Go!" Khia yelled as she looked in the rearview and saw the crazed man shooting at them. She couldn't see exactly who he was, but she wasn't trying to stick around and play Columbo either.

I thought the nigga was dead. Nautica scrambled to start the car and threw the shift in drive. As the terrifying sound of bullets thumping the car's exterior serenaded the girls, she sped off, ducking down slightly and peeking over the steering wheel, trying to merge into traffic. The way the bullets were coming, she knew it was an automatic weapon.

Nautica peeked into her rearview mirror again and saw Zion firing his gun. When she finally got far enough distance away for the bullets to stop hitting the car, she sat up and took a deep breath. Her heart beat rapidly, and she could barely drive straight because of her shaky hands.

After Nautica caught her breath, she tried to laugh it off. "Fuck him!" she yelled. "We did it!"

When Khia didn't respond, she looked over at her and saw her staring aimlessly, her head propped against the window. "Khia! Khia!" Nautica yelled. She reached over and shook Khia, and her body fell over, and her head flopped down on the dashboard, revealing a bloody hole in the back.

"No! Nooo!" Nautica yelled. "Don't die on me. We don't die! Khia!"

Nautica kept shaking Khia, but it was no use. The bullet had killed her on contact.

Nautica watched through the thick glass as the surgeons tried to revive Khia. She saw the doctor shake his head and signal for the staff to give up. He looked at the clock to get the time of death, and that's when Nautica's knees gave out. She fell to the ground and broke down crying like a newborn baby, her face buried in her hands. Khia was her first cousin, but they'd been like sisters. With neither of them having siblings, they naturally bonded with each other. She regretted taking the money, because it cost twenty-three year-old Khia her life.

After spending two hours at the hospital, Nautica decided to leave before the police came. She knew that carrying around eighty thousand dollars would make them suspicious. She clenched the bookbag. "Khia, I love you. I love you," she whispered in between cries.

Nautica pulled her shot-up Altima onto her aunt's block. She went to break the news to her—that her only child had been murdered. As she got close to the house, she noticed a black Charger parked three houses down from her aunt's home. She panicked when she saw the twenty-two-inch rims. *Oh shit! That looks like Loon's car.* She squinted to get a better look and saw Loon camped out in his car. She quickly sat Khia's gun on her lap and kept her eyes on Loon's car.

Nautica quickly turned into a driveway and got off the block before he noticed her. When she turned off the block, Loon's car hadn't moved. *Good. He didn't see me,* she thought as she got on the highway, tears of grief gracing her cheeks. She didn't know where she was headed, but she had to get out of Flint fast.

ME, MYSELF, AND A BAG OF MONEY

Chapter Eight

Nautica couldn't stop the tears from flowing as she pushed her car eighty miles per hour on the I-75. She hit the steering wheel. "Fuck!" she yelled, as images of Khia's dead body next to her emerged. She could still smell the blood, and it was driving her crazy. The wind coming through the broken glass in the back had her freezing as she drove to a destination unknown. Nautica didn't get a chance to see the shooter, but she assumed it was Zion. Her legs began to tremble. *How did he survive that? He's going to hunt me down.*

She drove and drove, not even paying attention to the road. It was as if she was letting the car drive itself. The only thing she had left was a bag full of money. Dirty money.

After hours of driving east, Nautica began to feel fatigue. She let out a big yawn. She decided that she'd still go to New York, just as she and Khia had planned. "I will figure out what to do when I get there," she said to herself.

Nautica thought about not being able to attend Khia's funeral, and about her mentioning being pregnant with Quaye's baby. She had tried to call her aunt, but always hung up when her aunt answered. How was she supposed to tell her that her only daughter had died? That she ran out of town like a coward?

Nautica entered the city limits of Chicago and got off on Halsted Avenue. Tired and confused, she decided to get a room for the night. When she saw the string of run-down motels, she decided against checking into a hotel right in the middle of the hood with a bag full of money. Nautica looked down at the dashboard. The dial was on *E*. "Damn!" She yawned and wiped her eye. It was too late to stop, and she didn't want to get out of the car at a random gas station with so much money on her.

She drove until she hit a main road with commercial suites. After fifteen minutes of searching, she found a Marriott Hotel. She glanced down at the clock and noticed it was 4:00 A.M. She pulled into the hotel parking lot and grabbed the duffle bag and her suitcase from the trunk. The sight of

Khia's suitcase next to hers brought more pain to her. She quickly closed the trunk.

Nautica headed for the lobby. Once she entered the glass doors, she knew she'd made the right decision to check in there. The gigantic hotel was immaculate, with its shining marble floors, and a huge glass chandelier hung about eighty feet above the ground in the middle of the main floor. She tied up her jacket tighter to make sure she wasn't revealing herself and walked to the front counter.

"Hello, ma'am, and welcome to the Marriott. How may I help you?" The front desk clerk looked Nautica up and down and turned up his nose at her attire. He was sure she was a hooker, especially checking in so late.

"I want to get a room," Nautica said, her eyes bloodshot. The mixture of tiredness and crying her eyes out had her looking strung out.

"Well, we don't have any rooms under three hundred dollars a night, ma'am," he said snobbily. "Maybe you want to try down the street. They have sixty-dollar rooms at the Econo Lodge."

Nautica couldn't believe the clerk's audacity. She cleared her throat and cocked her hip to the side, her hand resting on it. "What in the hell is that supposed to mean? Just give me a damn room, okay," she said, trying her best to be cordial.

"Well, I just thought—"

Nautica threw up her hand. "Well, that's why you don't get paid to think, mister smart ass. Now, just give me a room for three nights." She reached into her bag and pulled out a rubber band full of cash, peeled off a thousand dollars, and placed it on the table.

The man's eyes expanded when he saw the cash. He was totally embarrassed. "No problem, ma'am." He scooped up the thousand dollars and punched some keys on his computer. "Your total is nine eighteen with tax. I need to see some identification so I can check you in."

Nautica looked around the empty lobby and then back at Mr. Smart Ass. "No, you don't need any identification." She peeled off another five hundred dollars and slipped it to him.

The man's eyes lit up. He glanced around to make sure his manager wasn't around. "I sure as hell don't!" He snatched the cash and stuffed it into his pocket. He reached back to get her room key. "Your room number is seven three one, miss. Enjoy your stay."

With that Nautica headed to her room. The only thing that could numb her pain at that moment was sleep.

LIFE AIN'T SWEETIE

Chapter Nine

The strong odor of gasoline filled the air when Nautica woke up from her peaceful slumber. As she slowly began to gain her vision and wake up, she saw the vague image of a man hovering over her. Her heart began to beat faster and faster as the man's face began to become clearer. It was Zion. He had found her in the hotel in a matter of twenty-four hours. *He found me, he found me!* Nautica couldn't believe what was happening. She saw Zion's midsection bandaged up, because he was only wearing a wifebeater. Nautica tried to scream, but her mouth was duct taped. *Oh my God! No!* She tried to get up and run, but couldn't move.

Zion had managed to creep in and tie thick ropes around her and the whole bed. He had a demonic look in his eyes as he doused her with gasoline.

"Bitch, you thought you could just rob me and leave me? Huh?!" He poured the remainder of the gasoline all over the bed and on her body, even splashing some straight in her face.

Nautica squinted, trying to stop the burning sensation in her eyes. A mixture of tears and gas flowed down her face as she squirmed violently. She tried to yell, "Zion, no! Stop! Please, stop!" but all you heard was muffled sounds.

Zion took a few steps back. The look in his eyes as he stared at Nautica was worth a thousand words. Hateful ones. Without saying a word, he pulled a matchbox from his pocket and walked toward the door. He opened the door and, just before walking out, threw the match, which instantly sent the room up in flames.

Nautica cried and squirmed, violently trying to free herself, but the ropes were too tight. She knew this was her end.

Nautica woke up in a cold sweat kicking and screaming. She stared around the room, and there was no fire and no one else in the room. She was having a nightmare. She looked under the pillow for the small gun she'd taken from Khia and held it tight. Paranoia had her mind playing tricks on her.

Nautica slowly stood up and took a deep breath of relief, tears streaming from her eyes. She walked over to the sink and splashed water in her face. "Get a grip on yourself, Nautica," she whispered. She turned on the light and walked back over to the bed. She reached under the bed and grabbed the bag of money she'd stolen from Zion. "Fuck this money!" she yelled. She threw the bag against the wall, causing the money to fly everywhere, and for a brief moment, it rained hundred-dollar bills in the hotel room.

As she watched the money fall, she knew life wouldn't be the same for her. She knew Zion wouldn't stop until he found her. The original plan was for her and Khia to go to a new city and start over, but now she was on her own and lost.

Nautica sat in the diner next to the Marriott she was staying in. She was looking at a map, trying to find the quickest route to New York. As she finished up her steak and eggs, she heard a man yelling. She glanced out the front window and saw a tall, slim, dark-skinned man in a cheesy silk shirt yelling at a petite girl. He grabbed the girl by the throat and then gave her a swift slap across the face. The girl turned her head in pain and fell to the ground. The man then stood over her and began barking orders. He shook his head from side to side then jumped into a Cadillac DTS. The young girl stood up and wiped the blood from her mouth as she watched her pimp pull off.

Nautica couldn't believe the close resemblance the light-skinned girl had with Khia. Her short black hair and big brown eyes were identical to Khia's. Nautica's heart fluttered as she remembered her recent loss. She looked at the girl's hot pink mini-skirt and halter top that displayed her flat stomach. Obviously, she was a prostitute. *That's a shame. That girl doesn't look a day over sixteen.*

Nautica looked at the bill the waitress left her. "Damn! Twenty-one dollars!" she said under her breath. She chuckled when she remembered she had eighty thousand in the Louis Vuitton bag next to her. She discreetly reached into it and peeled off two twenties from one of the stacks and threw it on the table.

Nautica exited the diner and headed next door to her room. She wondered where she would go to start a new life. *Maybe LA.* Just as she reached the hotel entrance, she saw the same young girl who'd just been abused sitting on the stoop and smoking a cigarette. Tears streamed down the young girl's face as she crossed her legs and shook them vigorously.

Normally Nautica would've minded her own business, but something drew her to the girl. "What's wrong, li'l mama?"

The young girl looked up and puffed her cigarette like a stressed-out veteran. She turned up her nose. "What the fuck does it matter to you?" She wiped her tears away.

"Damn! Was just asking." Nautica rolled her eyes and kept moving.

Just before she stepped in the door, the girl stopped her. "Hey! Hold on, I'm sorry. I just got so much going on. Hi, my name is Sweetie." She put out the cigarette and extended her hand.

Nautica wanted to dismiss the girl, but her resemblance to Khia softened her heart. She took a deep breath and shook the girl's hand. "Nautica." She smiled reluctantly.

"I know you saw what happened back there, huh," Sweetie said, a little embarrassed. "I saw you sitting in the front of the restaurant."

"Yeah, I saw that bullshit." Nautica put her head down, trying not to make a big deal of it. She didn't want to humiliate the girl anymore than she already was.

"Yeah, he doesn't mean any harm, though. He's actually a good guy. He just wants me to stay focused when I'm working, you feel me? He said I didn't make enough money today."

"Why do you let him do that?"

"I really don't know. I guess when you don't have anyone else, you tend to be loyal to the people that you do have, feel me?"

Sweetie's habit of saying "feel me" after every sentence was making Nautica nauseous. She talked very fast and Nautica could hear traces of Spanish in her speech. "No, I'm not talking about being a prostitute, because I don't hate on nobody's money. I used to be a stripper, so I'm not looking down on you. I'm talking about letting him take your money when you do all the work. You don't need a nigga to manage your money. Shit, you can do that!" Nautica snapped her head back.

Sweetie was surprised to hear Nautica's response. She was so used to people looking down on what she did, she never expected Nautica to understand the game.

"I never looked at it that way. But, shit, it hard out here on a ho. Those johns be crazy as hell. You need a pimp to have yo' back out here, feel me? This Chicago, and bitches get killed every day." Sweetie pulled out another cigarette and let hang from the corner of her mouth as she lit it.

Nautica took a seat next to her, and they began to talk, instantly clicking.

Sweetie sat Indian-style on Nautica's bed. "New York, huh? I never been outside of Chicago."

Nautica and Sweetie had been together all day, and it was nearing nightfall as they sat in the hotel room talking about everything under the sun. Nautica discovered that Sweetie was much wiser than her seventeen years and was a good person, just lost. Her mother and father had died at a young age, and she was forced into foster care, just like Nautica. And she'd been turning tricks since she was fourten. They were like two peas in a pod. It seemed as if fate had brought them together.

Sweetie positioned herself comfortably on the bed and scanned around the spacious room. "This is a nice-ass hotel room. I'm not used to shit like this. Every room I see usually looks like a damn dungeon a' something."

"Yeah. I'm out of here in the morning," Nautica said as she combed her hair in the mirror. "I can't wait until I find my new life and leave all the bullshit behind me." She smiled to herself. She looked in the mirror and saw Sweetie drop her head. "Oh, I'm sorry. Here I am talking about how my life is about to change when you still in the trap."

Nautica sat next to Sweetie. Nautica looked at the young girl in front of her and knew that her life had been corrupted at a young age.

"No, it's cool. My time will come soon. As soon as I save up enough dough, I'm out too. Hell, maybe you'll see me out in New York in a while." Sweetie faked a smile, knowing that day probably would never come.

Nautica noticed the needle marks on Sweetie's arm. Sweetie followed her eyes and quickly turned her arms to hide them.

Everything began to make sense to Nautica now. That was the pimp's way of controlling and manipulating her, as with most girls lost in the world of prostitution—Cloud the mind with drugs.

"You're only seventeen," Nautica whispered as she looked into the girl's eyes. Something in her heart couldn't let the girl go down the wrong path like she and Khia had done. Nautica thought saving Sweetie would gain redemption for Khia's death. She took a deep breath and gently grabbed the girl's hand. "Look, let's go grab something to eat on me, okay."

Not used to getting anything for free, Sweetie's eyes lit up. "You're going to pay for my food?"

"I got you," Nautica said with a smile as she got up. "I'ma jump in the shower, and then we will be out, okay."

"Okay. Thank you, Nautica," Sweetie said, smiling from ear to ear.

Nautica got in the shower and began to think about everything that had gone on the past couple of days. Tears flowed and cascaded down her body right along with the shower water. She promised herself at that moment that this was the beginning of a new chapter of her life.

She then thought about helping Sweetie, showing her the right way. While washing herself, she yelled out over the sounds of the running water to Sweetie, "Maybe, you can, you know, go out to New York with me. It would be fun, you know. Don't worry about the money. I'll put you up until you get yo' shit straight."

After five minutes of washing, Nautica turned off the water and stepped out the shower. She wrapped the terrycloth robe around her body and stepped out into the room, drying her hair with another towel. "So what do you say? You game?"

Nautica looked around when Sweetie didn't respond. She finally noticed that no one was in the room. "Sweetie?" she called out. Nautica's heart began to speed up. She rushed to the closet and opened up the closet doors and felt her knees almost buckle. The money was gone! Nautica began to look around the hotel room frantically. "Fuck!" She jetted out of the room. "Li'l thievin' bitch!" she yelled as she ran full speed into the lobby.

By this time, her towel had come off, and she was hot-tailing it through the lobby completely naked and her hair wild. She then looked through the front glass and saw Sweetie getting into a cab. "Bitch!" she yelled and darted outside, running like an Olympic sprinter. A butt-naked Olympic sprinter.

But she wasn't fast enough. Before she could reach Sweetie, the cab had already pulled off. Nautica looked around for another cab so she could follow the taxi, but the street was empty. "Fuck!!!" She fell to her knees and let out one big scream as she grabbed her head and looked into the sky, totally floored by the fact that she was so gullible.

After ten minutes of crying and on her knees, Nautica finally returned to the hotel, not caring that she was completely naked and in a daze. *I just let my whole life leave in that cab.* As she stormed through the hotel, all eyes in the lobby were on her. "What the fuck are y'all looking at?" she yelled.

All Nautica could do when she made it to her room was stare at the walls in a stage of disbelief. She heard a knock on the door. She quickly wrapped a towel around herself. "If it's that bitch,

I'ma kill her." She quickly opened the door. It was the hotel manager and a bellhop.

"Excuse me, ma'am," the small-framed middle-aged white man said, "but we have to ask you to leave the premises."

"What the hell do you mean, leave the premises? I already paid for a couple of nights here!"

"You have caused a disruption, and the other guests are appalled. You are going to have to leave within thirty minutes, or I will be forced to call the police. You are not even authorized to be in this room, ma'am. There is no record of you checking in. You must leave now." The manager and bellhop walked off, not even giving Nautica a chance to explain herself.

She yelled, "Fuck this hotel!" and slammed the door in total rage.

Nautica was all cried out and had no more tears to shed as she went over to the side of the bed where her open suitcase was. She began throwing her clothes in her suitcase, cussing herself and Sweetie out. Normally she would've put up more of a fight with the manager, but she wanted to hurry up and leave before the cops came since she'd been an accessory to attempted murder only twenty-fours earlier.

With no money and no plan, she packed up and left the hotel.

SQUARE ONE

Chapter Ten

Nautica sat in the diner sipping coffee, trying to figure out her next move. "I'm not going to cry anymore," she said to herself. "It doesn't get me anywhere, feeling sorry for myself. I gotta stay strong for Khia. I'm back at square one, but I'm still going to New York!" She couldn't help but feel stupid because of her costly mistake, leaving a total stranger alone with her bag full of cash. *I have to figure out something.* She looked through her purse for her cell phone. "Damn, that bitch took my phone too?" Nautica shook her head in disbelief. All she had was sixty dollars, which she had in her pocket. She saw the pistol in her bag. She almost forgot she had it. Nautica took one last look inside her purse, hoping that her cell phone would magically appear, when she ran across a man's business card.

Nautica whispered, "Benny Donovan?" She stared at the card, trying to jog her memory. Then it hit her. He'd made her an offer months before, when she went to Baltimore with Zion. With nothing to lose, she decided to give him a call. She gathered some change from her purse and walked over to the diner's payphone. She dialed the number and leaned against the wall waiting for a response. On the fourth ring someone picked up.

"Yo," someone answered.

The background was loud with people chattering, and Nautica could barely hear him. She put her finger in her ear. "Hello, I'm looking for Benny Donovan."

"This him. Who dis?" he said, yelling over the loud noise.

"Hi, this is Nautica. You met me in Baltimore, and you told me to give you a call when I was in town, ya know, for the casting of *The Wire*?"

"Oh, yeah. You the chick that was wearing Chanel with Louis, right?" he said half-jokingly.

Nautica let out a chuckle. "Yeah, that's me. I was wondering were you still . . ." Nautica couldn't get her answer out before he cut her off.

"Okay, look, there is a casting call in B-more on Friday. Be there!"

Nautica grabbed a napkin and a stick of lipstick to write down the information. "I'm there.

Where is it?" She scrambled to write down the information.

"It's at Mondawmin Mall at two P.M. sharp, a'ight! Peace!" he said and hung up.

Nautica took a deep breath, feeling a little better. She had exactly five days to get to Baltimore. She wanted so bad to call back home to her aunt, but what could she say to her?

Nautica walked back to her table and placed a dollar on the table to pay for her coffee and went to her car. It was just about midnight, and she was too tired to drive, so she decided she would head east the next morning. She nodded off right in the diner's parking lot, not wanting to spend her last bit of money on a hotel room. She needed it to carry her over until she got to Baltimore. Then she would go from there.

She had never done any acting in her life, but it was worth a shot. She only wished that Khia was there to go with her. She knew that if she wasn't an actress, she damn sure was about to become one. As soon as she laid her head on her headrest, it seemed like she was sound asleep.

The sun's rays hit Nautica's face as she squinted her eyes and looked around her car. She glanced at her clock and saw that it was 9:00 A.M. She had slept all night like a baby. She yawned and stretched her arms as much as she could inside her tiny car. She grabbed the map from her glove box and began to search for the best route to Baltimore.

After studying it for a few minutes, she started up the car and headed toward the freeway. The air from the busted window was irritating her as she shook her head and tried to ignore it, but she couldn't.

Just as she approached the highway, she felt her car begin to sputter. "Damn!" She'd been so taken up with everything going on, she forgot to put gas in the car. "I got to have the worst luck on earth, I swear!" Nautica yelled as her car completely shut off. She began to pound on the steering wheel. She got out of her car and began to kick her tires, releasing some of her tension.

She grabbed her purse out of her car and headed back down the road where the gas station was. It was about five miles back, and the way the sun was beaming, she knew she had a torturous journey ahead of her. She walked on the side of the road, trying to balance herself in her six-inch heels, reflecting on her life. Everything had changed for her in the last couple of days. Within minutes, she was sweaty and tired. The blistering sun had her feeling like she was in a microwave. Nautica pulled off her top shirt, because it had gotten so soaked, and wiped her forehead with it. Underneath, she wore a small tank top. She saw the distant BP gas station sign down the road. As Nautica walked down the rocky road, she heard a car approach her and then a male's voice.

"'Ey, baby. You need to come work for me, baby. I'm here to treat you, not beat you. So gon' 'head an' get in the car with Silk," the man said, talking about himself in third person. He thought she was a working girl because of her small tank top and six-inch heels.

Oh my goodness, this nigga thinks I'm a mu'fuckin' hooker. Nautica didn't even extend him the courtesy of looking at him and began to speed up her walk. She just lowered her head and tried her best to ignore his lame lines.

"Look, babygirl, I'm what you need. I am going to the moon and if you wanna go with me, the only thing you have to do is get in. Yo' square-ass pimp got you out here on the track. You need to be in a luxury suite making yo' paper, baby."

Nautica was fed up with him and his corny lines that seemed to come straight out of *The Mack*, and was about to tell him about himself. She stopped and put her hands on her hips as she looked at him, but when she saw the black Cadillac and the man's face, she thought, *Ain't that a bitch! It's Sweetie's pimp. I can't believe this shit.* Her smile quickly turned into a frown.

The man stopped his car and grinned, displaying his gap-toothed smile. His teeth had a yellow coloration in them across the top, and Nautica almost gagged at the sight of them.

He leaned toward the passenger side and ran his hand over his stubble. "So what do you say, sweetness? Wanna go to the moon, or you want to keep walking on this hot-ass track with no direction?"

"Sounds like a plan." Nautica tried to do her best hooker impersonation as she strutted to his car and hopped in, knowing he would lead her to Sweetie and her money. She tried her best not to laugh at his corny ass. She stared at his gaps and the way he kept smiling. *He sho' ain't trying to hide that ugly-ass grill of his.* She ran her fingers through her hair and got comfortable.

"My name is Silk, baby. What's yours?" He stared at Nautica's thighs. He was in pimp paradise. He couldn't believe that he'd snagged a beauty like Nautica so easily.

Looking at his yellow teeth, she answered, "They call me Butter," saying the first thing that came to her mind. She almost laughed at her own joke.

Silk licked his lips and continue to rub his facial hair, trying to be debonair. "How you get a name like that, baby? You look like a caramel or something like that. Well, anyway, you've made the right choice today, baby."

As soon as he pulled off, he placed his hands on Nautica's inner thigh. Nautica jumped at his touch, but quickly caught herself and smiled. She parted her legs slightly, trying to be cooperative enough not to turn him away. She looked at his clothes. He had on beige slacks with a bright yellow shirt. The outfit wasn't so bad, but it was the way he wore it and accessorized that turned Nautica off. He had his top three buttons undone, displaying his nappy chest hair, and to top it off, he had the nerve to wear a small gold cross that seemed to get lost in the bush that rested on his upper body. Nautica looked down at his feet, and just as she expected, he had on gators, yellow ones.

Nautica moved his hand discreetly, not wanting to show her disgust, and began to rub the dash. "Ooh, I like this leather interior," she said in a fake Southern accent. "Down in Texas, we don't see cars like this very often."

"You from big Texas, huh?"

"Yea, I came up here with my girlfriend to make a better life for myself," Nautica lied, saying whatever popped into her head. Actually she was having fun toying with Silk.

"Is that right? Well, look, baby, I got plenty more where this came from. You ain't seen nothing yet. I'ma take real good care of you, understand?" Silk smiled. He'd hit a gold-mine by having a woman from out of town. That meant she had no family members in town to interfere with his brainwashing.

"Okay, daddy." She smiled.

SWEETEST REVENGE

Chapter Eleven

Nautica and Silk pulled up to a medium-sized brick house. Nautica's palms sweated. She hoped that Sweetie was in there. Just the thought of seeing her had Nautica anxious. She was prepared to give her the worst ass-whupping imaginable before taking her money back. *I hope this bitch is in here.* She reached inside her purse and felt the small caliber pistol. She had no idea how to use it, but she knew it couldn't be too hard.

Silk had been running his game on her the whole way to his home, but Nautica didn't pay attention to him the entire drive. All she could think about was getting to Sweetie. She nodded and smiled occasionally, but everything he said to her fell on deaf ears. She wanted to ask about Sweetie when she first got in the car, but she didn't know if he knew about the caper, so she held her cards.

"Come on into the palace." Silk stepped out of the car and hurried around to open the door for Nautica. He was still awed by her beauty. She was by far the most beautiful girl he ever had on his roster. *This bitch gon' make me rich*. He closed the door and then smacked Nautica on the ass.

As he led her up to his front door, his cell phone began to ring. He placed the phone in between his shoulder and ear, so that he could have free hands to open the door. "Speak," he said.

Nautica tried to listen close, wondering if it was Sweetie on the other end.

Silk opened the door and let Nautica in. He flicked on the light and displayed his living room. The red carpet resembled a showroom floor at the MGM Grand Casino, and the lava lamps and red furniture only added insult to injury.

Silk smiled proudly as he listened closely to the person on the other end of the phone. He smacked Nautica once again on her behind. He held up one finger to signal that he would be off the phone shortly.

Nautica slowly walked in and sat on the couch.

Silk faded into the back of the house. He shouted into the phone, "Bitch, you ain't checked in in twenty-four hours! Sweetie, you betta bring that ass home!" He held the phone close to his mouth as if it was a walkie-talkie.

Nautica's eyes lit up at the sound of Sweetie's name. She stood up and walked by the hallway that led to the room where Silk had gone. She wanted to hear what he was saying.

"Look, bitch, I don't care what lick you came up on. You betta have yo' ass home in thirty minutes, or I'ma beat yo' ass when I catch you! Try me!"

Nautica heard the click from him flipping down his cell phone and quickly returned to her seat. Silk appeared just as she sat down.

"Sorry about that, but you know how the game go. Bitches ain't got no 'act-right' these days, feel me?" He sat on the couch next to Nautica.

Nautica inched away from him when she smelled his cheap cologne. "It's cool. You have other workers?" She wanted to find out more about Sweetie.

"Well, I just have one bitch right now, but with you on the team, the sky is the limit, feel me?"

Nautica realized where Sweetie got the habit of saying, "Feel me," after every statement.

Silk grabbed both of Nautica's hands and looked into her eyes. She couldn't stand the look in his eyes. His eyes partially stuck out of his eye sockets, making him almost resemble a Simpson.

"Look, Butter, you are in safe hands now, and any and everything you know about the ho business, you need to forget. I'ma teach you how to work a john out until he is completely bone-dry. See, my girls send their johns home back to the wife broke and full of hope, hoping that their wife can do what one of my girls had just done to them. See, most chicks look at the bulge in the middle of a man's pants to see what they're packing. But, see, my girls are taught to look in the bulge on the side of their pants, their money bulge, feel me? That's how you got to think. Every man is a potential cash cow and victim. Are you catching all of this?"

Nautica nodded her head. She was just waiting for Sweetie to show up. *This dude is a clown. I know this isn't what he called game. He needs to find another profession, straight up. Where is this bitch at?*

"I see you a quiet one, huh?" Silk looked at Nautica's body with the bedroom eyes. He threw his arm around her and slowly stroked her shoulder. He was hot and ready to try out his own product before putting it out on the street.

Nautica knew she had to hold him off until Sweetie got there. *I know this greasy-ass nigga better take his hands off of me. Sweetie need to bring her ass on, so I can pistol whip that thieving ass . He can get it too if he tries to jump in.* She put on a fake smile and ran her fingers through her hair.

Silk slid his hand down to her breasts, and she despised every minute of it. He slipped one breast out of her shirt and bent down and put it in his mouth.

"Hold up," Nautica said, easing back.

"Come on, Butta, don't be afraid." Silk momentarily glanced at her.

The sound of a car pulling into Silk's driveway reached their ears. "Hold that thought." He got up and peeked through his blinds. "Who the hell is that?" he whispered to himself. He squinted his eyes and to see who was driving the Benz into his driveway.

Moments later he saw Sweetie step out in a mink coat and new shoes. He got enraged as he came to the conclusion that Sweetie had "chose," which meant another pimp snatched his girl. "Oh, hell naw!" he exclaimed, a look of disbelief on his face.

"Who is that?" Nautica put her breast back into her top.

"Just gimme a minute. That's my other girl. I gotta handle something real quick, so just sit tight," he said, lines forming in his forehead.

Just as Silk made his way to the door to meet Sweetie, Nautica reached into her purse for the gun. "I have to use the ladies room," she said.

Silk peeked out of his screen door. "Yeah, whatever," he said, waving her off. "It's in the back." He was ready to beat the hell out of Sweetie for disrespecting him and driving another man's car to his house.

Actually Sweetie had gone to the used Mercedes dealership and copped it with $20,000 cash earlier that day, and wanted to surprise him with it.

Nautica stood up and made her way to the back room, so Sweetie wouldn't notice her when she came in. She slipped into the bathroom and closed the door just enough to still see Silk.

Silk yanked Sweetie up by her hair as soon as she stepped through the door. "What the fuck is your problem, bitch?! Who car is that?!"

Nautica saw Sweetie drop Zion's Louis bag on the floor as Silk slapped her around like a rag doll. "Damn," she whispered.

"Daddy, I got some mon—"

"Bitch, shut up!" He threw her against the wall, causing the lamp to fall and break. He then walked over to her, grabbed her by the hair, and dragged her to the back room.

Sweetie continued to yell for him to stop, but it didn't help. She was trying to tell him about the money in between her cries, but he wasn't trying to hear anything. The only thing on his mind was her being gone for a whole day and coming back with fancy clothes and a Mercedes Benz.

Nautica quickly closed the bathroom door as they brushed past her. She heard another door slam and then the sound of arguing. She ran into the living room and grabbed the bag off the floor. She opened it up, and the money was still there, some of it at any rate. She glanced at the table and saw the keys to the Benz laying there. She grabbed them up and hurried out of the door. She jumped into the Benz, started the car, and listened as the luxury car purred. Then she smoothly pulled off in her new Benz, smiling from ear to ear. She had just been reunited with her favorite man in the world. Benjamin Franklin.

AMERICAN DREAMIN'

Chapter Twelve

Nautica gripped the woodgrain steering wheel and rode down the freeway going east toward Baltimore. She smiled as she looked around the car and its leather interior. Sweetie had left the car title in the glove compartment, like a dumb ass, so Nautica knew she had just got a new car. Her smile eventually turned into a pained look as she remembered how she and Khia always talked about their first Benz.

She began talking to herself, trying to sort out her thoughts about her next move.

"Now that I got the money, I'm good. I am about to go to Baltimore and get on my shit, watch!" she said, trying to convince herself that everything was okay. She looked down at the navigational screen that sat just above the CD player. She had set it to lead her straight to Baltimore. She still planned on going to the open audition that the casting director invited her to, because by the way the bag felt, she knew that Sweetie had spent a nice chunk of the money.

Nautica couldn't shake the thought of her dead cousin, though. No matter how hard she tried, tears seemed to keep coming. "My heart hurts. But I know you are up there watching me, bitch." She smiled. Khia and her used to always call each other bitches good-naturedly. Nautica had never thought so much about the little things they shared. *I'ma be okay and I'm still going to live out our dream, K.*

Nautica felt as if she had an angel with her, and she promised herself and Khia that she would have the American dream, just like they had planned before Khia's untimely demise.

Nautica made it to the place where the auditions were being held. She walked through the mall with confidence, rocking her tight Dior jeans with a white bebe shirt, and the heels had her behind sitting upright and perfect for the viewing eye. She had her hair pulled back tightly, and her soft baby hair rested flawlessly around her edges. She felt alive again, as she hid behind the black Dolce & Gabbana shades. She had stopped at a couple malls along the way to Baltimore to get fresh and, yes, she was fresh to death.

She'd counted the money and discovered that she had just about $55,000 left. She couldn't believe Sweetie had spent close to $25,000 in a day's time, but she was grateful that she at least got some of the money back. The Mercedes Benz wasn't too shabby either.

As Nautica got closer to the middle of the mall, where all the cameras were, she saw a long line of females waiting to get auditioned. Her heart dropped as she saw the hundreds of girls waiting to take her part. *Oh, hell naw.* She stopped in her tracks. She took her place in line as she got prepared for a long wait. A very long wait.

A girl with a ghetto weave job and long fake nails said, "Girl, I got this shit. It's a wrap! As soon as they see me, I'ma get the part." She wrapped her gum around her finger and continued to talk loudly to her friend in front of her in the line.

Nautica looked the girl up and down. *Bitch, please.* She kept thinking about the money in her trunk. She had to hurry up and get back to it. She didn't want to lose it again.

Nautica had been in line for about two hours and was now only three people back from the start of the line. She had been looking over the small script that one of the directors had given every girl. The paper only had five lines on it, which she memorized within fifteen minutes. She smiled as she saw Benny sitting next to the director auditioning the girls. He didn't see her in line, but Nautica knew that once he saw her again, she would get the part.

The ghetto girl in front was still talking loud. "Yeah, girl, I got this shit." She looked at herself in her pocket-sized mirror. "Benny Donovan, the casting director, gave me a personal invitation." She whipped out the same business card that Nautica had.

Fuck! Nautica wasn't feeling so special any more. She shook her head and looked over her line one last time.

"That's it!" a white man said, waving his arms. "That's a wrap! Auditions are over." He hopped out of his chair.

Nautica's jaws dropped as she looked around in confusion, and an abundance of displeased sighs and mumbles erupted from the rest of the girls in line.

The ghetto girl in front of Nautica in the line began to throw a fit. "What the fuck you mean, that's a wrap? Wrap my ass!" she yelled. "I have been standing here for two hours! Somebody gon' audition me!" She threw her hands on her hip and waved her arm in the air, snapping and jerking her neck.

Nautica threw both of her hands in the air. She had driven all the way to Baltimore for nothing. She threw the paper with the lines on it onto the floor and stormed off.

Her heels clicking the floor got Benny's attention. He saw her profile as she turned to leave. "Yo, hold up," he said to the producer as he ran after Nautica. "We got one more audition!"

Nautica looked back and saw Benny coming after her.

"Hold up, ma!" he said as he approached her. "I thought you weren't coming." Benny led her back to the video shooting area. "Let's see what you got."

The same ghetto girl stepped out of line and in their path. "Why that bitch get to audition? I was in line before her!"

Benny yelled, "Security!" and just like that, two bulky, cock-diesel men escorted her out of the building kicking and screaming.

Nautica smiled and walked past the other girls. *Here goes nothing,* she thought as she walked in front of the director to show him what she could do.

"You did great," Benny said as he sat down with Nautica at the food court.

Nautica smiled and sipped on her milk shake, feeling antsy inside. She knew she did well by the way the directors' faces lit up after her audition. They'd told her on the spot that she had the part. "Thanks," she said, trying not to sound too excited.

"We will go over the paperwork tomorrow morning." Benny dug into the Chinese food in front of him.

Nautica shook her head. She studied Benny's appearance. She couldn't see herself being more than friends with him. She wasn't feeling the pretty boy S-curl and the manicured fingernails. She agreed to have lunch with him just because he was the reason she got the part. She would play the stripper girlfriend of one of the corner boys on the show. It was a small role, but it paid $10,000 an episode, which was good money to Nautica.

"Benny, I just want to say thank you again for the opportunity. You really looked out."

"It's all good. You have a lot of talent, and you have a face for television." He made a rectangle with his hands around her face as if she was on a television screen. "But, look, let's celebrate." He wiped his hands with a napkin. "Everyone from the set is going out tonight and partying just before we start filming. You game?"

Nautica said as she lit up, knowing that the stars of the show would be in attendance. "Yeah, I'm down."

"Cool. I'm going to introduce you to some directors and heavy people in the business. A lot of movie stars and filmmakers are going to be there. It's a good way to network. It's a very exclusive event."

"Cool." Nautica was beginning to like Baltimore more and more by the minute. She'd only been there for a couple of hours, and already she'd landed an acting job and an invite to an industry party.

"Here is the address. Meet me there at ten." Benny wrote an address on a napkin. "It's a white party." He got up, dropped a hundred-dollar bill on the table for a tip, and walked out.

Nautica smiled as she watched Benny walk away. *I could get used to this.* She put the napkin in her purse along with the hundred-dollar bill he'd left for the waitress. "I'll take that." She slid the bill into her purse.

THE WHITE PARTY

Chapter Thirteen

Nautica pulled up to the loading dock's parking lot, where the bright lights that shined from the huge yacht captivated everyone's attention. She saw people loading the dock from the long red carpet that led up to it.

She had gotten a hotel room near the Inner Harbor in Baltimore, a place she decided to call her home until she knew her next move. She'd stood in the hotel's mirror for hours to get just right for the spectacle, and she knew she was the shit that night. She took a deep breath and gave herself one last look in her visor's mirror to make sure her shit was intact.

Nautica stepped out and graced the pavement with her brand-new Manolo Blahnik. She pulled down her small black dress that attempted to rise up. Lines of luxury cars occupied the spacious car lot, which looked like a Mercedes dealer's lot, with all the Benzes lined next to each other. Her heart began to speed up as she approached the ladder that led to the boat, as all the lights overwhelmed her. *I couldn't get used to this.* She made her way up to the yacht and approached the man with a clipboard who stood at the top of the ladder. She smiled and said, "Nautica Fairfax."

The big brawny guy ran his index finger down the list. He flipped the page and repeated the same thing, mumbling. After a couple of seconds he looked at her and shook his head from side to side. "Sorry, ma. Your name isn't on the list."

"Are you sure? It's Nautica Fairfax." Nautica said as she took a glance at his list for him.

He quickly pulled the clipboard close to his chest and shook his head no. Nautica cocked her hip to the side, trying to show him her full figure. He took a glance at the pretty sight, but he wasn't falling for it. He continued to shake his head and began to wave other people to come up past her.

"This some bullshit," Nautica whispered. She turned to head back down the stairs. She was so embarrassed because people had to step aside to let her down. It was like the walk of shame.

"Yo, Nautica! Nautica!" a man's voice called.

Nautica turned around and saw Benny waving for her to come up. He was standing right next to the same man who'd told her she wasn't on the list. She smiled and headed back up the stairs.

When Nautica reached the top of the stairs again, Benny, a bottle of Moët in his hands, took a look at her up and down. "Hey, what's going on?" He wrapped one arm around her.

"Hey, Benny." Nautica brushed past the doorman and gave him a menacing stare. She followed Benny up another set of stairs, wraparound stairs made of glass, that sat in the middle of the deck. She'd never seen anything like it.

They reached the beautiful, gigantic dance floor at the top, where people were two-stepping to the sounds of R. Kelly and the place was crowded. The sub woofers let out a crisp sound of harmony as everyone was dancing and having a great time.

Benny looked Nautica up and down and giggled loudly.

"What's so funny?" Nautica nervously pulled down her dress and looked at herself.

"No, it's nothing. I just see you decided to be different, huh?" He brushed off his white linen shirt with his free hand.

Nautica began to see a trend. She looked around and noticed everyone seemed to be wearing white. She had fucked up. She'd been so nervous, she hadn't even noticed. *A white party*, she said in her head. She put her hand over her face in embarrassment and began to laugh. She thought that meant that the party was going to be full of Caucasian people. "Oh my God."

"It's cool." Benny grabbed a flute glass of wine from the tray of a passing waiter and handed it to Nautica.

Nautica graciously accepted it and downed it just as quick as she got it. She needed something to loosen her up, get her more relaxed.

"Let's go in the VIP section so I can introduce you to some people." Benny extended his forearm so Nautica could latch on. She wrapped her arm around his, and he led her to the back of the gigantic yacht.

The back section was sectioned off by velvet ropes and had its own bar and bartender. Mostly everyone in the section had their own bottle of champagne in their hand, and most of the attention was toward the back, where a group of men sat.

Benny led Nautica to the bar and ordered a bottle of Grey Goose. Nautica sat next to him and slowly sipped from her flute glass. She noticed a group of girls focusing their attention on one particular man, who sat in the middle of the entourage. The man didn't pay any mind to the woman who danced seductively around him, obviously trying to get his attention. Nautica knew instantly he was someone important.

The men in his entourage were drooling over the woman, but he acted as if they weren't even there, just slowly bobbing his head and sipping on the bottle of Moët in his hand.

Nautica kept her eye on him as Benny tried to spark small talk with her. She was trying to listen to Benny, but her attention was on the man that seemed to be so important.

Benny noticed that Nautica's attention was on the crowd in the corner. He glanced at them and then back at her. "That's Tical Manny," he said, grabbing the Grey Goose bottle and cracking it open. He took a sip of the liquor. "He is a financial backer for the show. He helped pay for it, before the network picked it up. He's real tight with the creator of the show."

"Oh, yeah?" Nautica couldn't keep her eyes off of him. She was surprised to hear he was a part of the show; he didn't seem like that type.

Tical was young and had a rugged look. His facial hair laid on his face perfectly, yet wildly. His five o'clock shadow reminded her of the rapper Jim Jones. He wore a crisp white Polo shirt with white linen pants, and his white fitted cap was pulled down just above his thick, dark eyebrows, barely displaying his hazel brown eyes. His brown skin was sort of an almond color. He had on a platinum chain that hung to his belt buckle that totally outshined any piece of jewelry on the boat. He gave off an aura that screamed *power*.

Nautica was feeling him and definitely wanted to learn more. She stopped staring and focused her attention on Benny. She caught a glimpse of his manicured nails and wondered if he was gay. Usually her "gaydar" was on point, and though she really couldn't tell with Benny, she had her suspicions.

A butch-looking female with cornrows, about five foot four, walked over to Benny with an extended hand. She wore an all-white tee with baggy jeans. She slowly pulled up her sagging pants. "What's good, Benny?" The woman slapped palms with Benny.

"What's good, Scoop?" Benny embraced her.

"Ain't shit. What's been going on?" she asked in her deep Baltimore accent.

"Nothing. Just getting ready for filming to start." Benny turned to Nautica. "Yo, I want you to meet Nautica. She's going to be playing the love interest of one of the corner boys this season. Nautica, this is Scoop. She's going to have a big role this season."

Scoop looked at Nautica up and down and slowly began to rub her hands together. She had such a heavy thug demeanor, Nautica briefly forgot she was a girl.

"What's good, ma?" Scoop continued to stare at Nautica's shape.

"Hello." Nautica extended her hand. She quickly turned her attention back to the bar and took a sip of her drink. She didn't want Scoop to think she swung that way.

"Yo, listen, we about to blow a spliff on the roof," Scoop said to Benny. "You coming?" She pulled out a bag of lime-green Kush from her pocket.

Benny put on a big smile and nodded his head. He followed the weed as if it was a pendulum being held by a hypnotist. "Yeah. You smoke, Nautica?"

Nautica wasn't a heavy smoker, but she wanted to mingle and not throw a wrench in the plans. "Yeah, a little," she said as she stood up off the bar stool.

They all went up to the roof on the vacant third level with perfectly polished wooden floors and running Jacuzzi in the center. The vibration of the music from the bottom floor thumped against their feet as they walked to the edge of the boat and stool by the rails of the ship.

Nautica stared at the big ocean that lay before her, and inhaled the invigorating fresh air.

The moon's glow shined brightly and created a purple hue that bounced off the massive water, and the sound of the waves created a relaxing melody.

Scoop began to twist up the smoke, her eyes on Nautica, but Nautica continued to stare out into the ocean, while Benny stood next to her downing his liquor.

"Here." Benny attempted to hand Nautica the bottle of liquor, but Nautica put her hand up, not wanting to get too drunk in the midst of so many people she didn't know.

She stood there looking at the ocean as Benny and Scoop conversed. She saw right through Benny. He was corny and boastful. She quit listening after the fifth time he mentioned his fleet of Benzes.

Benny pulled a couple red pills out of his pocket and slipped one to Scoop. He thought he was being slick about it, but Nautica saw when he went into his pocket. She immediately knew they were ecstasy pills.

Nautica took a deep breath and turned her head, like she didn't see him pass it. *I don't know what kind of party this nigga thinks it is. But he's got another thing coming.* She rolled her eyes. She wanted to leave her past life in Flint. She didn't want to start rolling again.

She felt hands go up her dress and quickly turned around and slapped them away. Scoop had tried to rub her vagina. Nautica looked over at Benny, thinking he would have interjected, but he was holding his crotch and staring at her body.

Scoop inched closer to Nautica. "Come on, ma. Don't be shy."

Nautica placed her hand on Scoop's small-breasted chest, to stop her from invading her personal space. "Back the fuck up. I don't get down like that." She glanced at Benny, waiting for him to jump in, but instead he grabbed her behind.

"Man, I thought you said she was a jump-off." Scoop waved her hand in dismissal and headed toward the stairs.

Benny became more aggressive and grabbed Nautica by the waist, pulling her close to him. Nautica tried to push him away, but Benny was too strong. She felt his tongue on her neck.

"Stop, Benny!" Nautica yelled. "Stop, mu'-fucka!" She smacked the shit out of him.

Benny immediately looked at her like she was crazy. "You li'l ghetto bitch. I'm the one who got you the part and you acting like a bitch?" He cocked his hand back, and Nautica flinched and closed her eyes.

Out of nowhere a hand came and grabbed Benny.

"What the fuck?" Benny turned around to fight whoever was getting into his business, but his attitude quickly changed when he saw the hazel eyes looking down at him.

Nautica opened her eyes and saw the same man she'd noticed earlier releasing Benny's arm. The hazel-eyed man had another muscular man standing next to him, both of them staring at Benny.

"You drunk, Benny. Yo, Gunplay," he said calmly, displaying his charming smirk.

"Yeah." The well-built man stepped up closer to Benny.

"Show this nigga the door. He needs to go home and sleep that liquor off."

Benny looked back at Nautica and then back at the man. He straightened up his collar. "You right, Tical." He started to walk toward the stairs, Gunplay escorting him.

Tical placed his hand on Benny's chest and stopped him in his tracks. "You forgetting something." He threw his head in the direction of Nautica, who was fixing her dress.

"Oh, yeah." He turned toward Nautica and began to walk up on her with an apologetic face. "Nautica, I'm sorry abo—"

Nautica didn't give him a chance. She gave him a firm smack to the side of his face that echoed throughout the top deck, and left a handprint on Benny's face, which instantly became red.

Gunplay let out a small chuckle. "Shorty ain't playing no games," he said, instigating.

Benny's reaction was totally different from the way he acted when she'd smacked him the first time. He just bowed his head and turned around to leave.

Nautica shook her head in disgust. She then focused on the handsome man that stood before her. She knew he was an important person, from the way Benny reacted to him. She tried to straighten up her hair. "Thank you,"

"It ain't nothing. You good?"

"Yeah, I'm okay. I don't know what's wrong with that fool. I don't get down like that."

"Don't trip. Benny just gets stupid sometimes. I'm Tical. So what's your name?"

The man stared into Nautica's eyes. He didn't smile, but he had a softness that shined through his beautiful hazel eyes. He had a small teardrop tattooed just under his right eyelid, which Nautica found very attractive.

"I'm Nautica." Nautica extended her hand. She realized she was still frowning from Benny's actions and quickly straightened her face up. She shook his hand and quickly turned around. She regretted slapping Benny. She knew she'd just blown her chance at the acting role. She stared into the ocean, totally ignoring the man behind her.

Tical joined her and looked into the ocean also. "What's wrong?"

"Nothing. You wouldn't understand anyway."

"How do you know?" he asked, his eyes on the water. "Tell me."

"I just flushed my job down the drain. He just hired me for a role in the show, and now I'm done." Nautica ran her fingers through her hair.

"I don't think you're going to be having any problem with Benny, trust me."

"How are you so sure?"

"I just know, trust me. He was just a little drunk. I'll talk to him in the morning." Tical licked his lips and focused on Nautica's eyes. "So how do you like the party?"

"It's cool, I guess. I really like this yacht." Nautica ran her hands over the steel rails. "I know something like this cost a lot of money."

"Yeah, just under a half million," Tical answered with his low, raspy voice. He spoke very low, but clearly and evenly.

"How you know? You into boats or something?"

"Yeah, kinda. I should know. I bought it."

Nautica began to blush. She took another look at him, and her attraction to him before, multiplied by ten. "Are you serious?"

"Yeah, I'm serious." Tical showed his flawless smile, except for the very tiny gap between his two front teeth, which some women find adorable. "I'm kind of a big deal around here," he said, his eyes stuck on Nautica's.

"Oh, you the man, huh?"

"No, I'm just playing. I'm just a regular dude," he said, self-assured.

"You don't seem so regular to me." Nautica picked up the diamond and platinum chain off his chest.

"I see you like to be different, huh?"

"What you mean by that?"

Tical pointed at her dress, pointing out that she was wearing all black at an all-white party.

Nautica giggled and put her hand over her mouth. "It was a little misunderstanding." She shared a laugh with him. "So what do you do to afford a big boat like this?" She knew it had to be something extravagant because, where she was from, a dopeman might have a luxury car, but not a luxury boat, and so she dismissed the thought of him being a hustler. *He must come from a rich family or something. Or maybe he's an athlete.*

"I'm into the stock market. I had a lot of luck in investing."

Tical didn't want to tell her the whole truth. Well, actually he didn't lie. He was an investor in the streets, and it paid him handsomely. He was the boss of the streets of Baltimore, hands down. His name put fear in niggas' hearts, and he could make the realest nigga feel like a bitch. His business savvy was legendary in the city, and that's what actually drew him to the show when it first went into production. He knew the show would be special and invested early, which turned out to be a great power move for him. Now he had an income that could potentially clean his money and enable him to go legit.

Ice broken, Nautica and Tical had a two-hour conversation over a bottle of Moët.

It wasn't long before she discovered Tical's humility and intelligence. He was well-educated, but hood. Nautica was impressed. Tical was far from what she was used to in Flint, where she always had it one way or the other. When she started to like street niggas, they turned out to be dumb as hell, and when she dated intelligent brothers, they wasn't hood enough for her. Tical had the perfect balance. She loved the way he took his time before every statement, as if he strategically put his words together to roll off his tongue to make perfect sense every time. His deep baritone sent chills down her back.

Tical and Nautica were laughing and enjoying each other's company so much, neither of them realized that the party was over until they went downstairs to an empty dance floor.

Gunplay was at the bar drinking, talking to the bartender as he wiped the countertop. Tical and Nautica walked up to him as he downed a shot of vodka.

"Tical, there you are." Gunplay looked at Tical with drunken eyes. "I didn't see you all night, my nigga." He looked over at Nautica. "You kept my man pretty busy."

She smiled as she looked at Tical and thought about the great conversation they shared all night.

Tical nodded toward his friend. "This is my man, Eric Murdock, but we call him Gunplay."

"Nice to meet you, Gunplay." Nautica extended her hand. "That's a helluva name."

"It's a childhood nickname that just stuck," Gunplay lied, knowing he got the name because of his murder game.

Gunplay was a killer, point-blank and simple. He had rocked more people to sleep than a nursery, and his name also rang bells in the streets. He was Tical's right-hand man, and they were the perfect combination of brains and muscle. While so-called real niggas were smoking blunts in the middle of a street war, he was smoking niggas, and that kept Tical's operation on top.

"I'ma walk her to her car, fam. I'll be right back." Tical placed his arm on the small of Nautica's back.

"Nice meeting you," Nautica said to Gunplay, and she and Tical headed toward the steps to exit the yacht.

Nautica clinched her small purse when she reached her car. "I guess this is it, huh?"

Tical was used to girls having broken-down hoopties that tried to get at him. *It seems like she got her shit together*, he thought, not knowing that just a couple days before she was driving a busted-down Honda.

"Yeah, I guess it is. It was a pleasure." Tical reached for Nautica's hand. They shook hands, and Tical gently pulled her closer to him.

Nautica could smell the fresh scent of Tical's cologne as she closed her eyes and rested her forehead on his chest.

"This night can't end . . . not yet, at least," Tical said almost in a whisper. He looked down at Nautica and kissed the top of her head.

"You know what," Nautica responded, "I was thinking the same thing," and she melted into his arms.

Nautica sped through the Baltimore highway trying to keep up with Tical's smoke-colored drop-top Cadillac XLR. The car sat so close to the ground, it looked as if it was floating across the pavement. She laughed hysterically as she tried to keep up with the speedy vehicle.

Tical periodically peeked at her through his rearview mirror and smiled at her. He'd told her to follow him, and he decided to play a little cat-and-mouse game.

Nautica felt the torque in her new car and loved the way it handled. She pushed the button that dropped the top to her car, so Tical could see her face as she stayed on his ass.

Tical smiled as he glanced back at Nautica and saw the "let her titties show," a term used to describe a topless car. He saw her long hair flowing in the wind and loved the way it made her look. Tical saw his exit coming and quickly switched three lanes over to get off.

Nautica, thinking fast, switched right with him and got off too. She couldn't stop laughing. She was having the time of her life. She felt so lawless, so free, and so alive. Her heart beat fast as the adrenaline pumped through her body.

Nautica slowed her car and followed Tical to an oversized tri-level manor on the outskirts of Baltimore. Tical had invited her to his house, and she couldn't turn down the offer. The house was a couple hundred yards from the water and had its own entrance that sat on the oceanfront. "This is beautiful," she said as she followed Tical's car to the parking area near the beach.

He was the first to hop out, and then Nautica did, her hand on her chest. "My heart is beating so fast," she said, "I never drove that fast in my entire life."

He smiled as he waited for her to walk over. "You can handle the wheel pretty good. I thought I was going to shake you."

"I know how to handle mine."

"Welcome to my home." Tical waved at his gorgeous place. He took off his shoes and began to walk on the sand. "Come on."

Nautica took off her heels and followed him. The sand felt good between her toes as they made the way to the back entrance of the house.

"That house is beautiful," Nautica admired the glass house that lit up so nicely against the darkness. The house was like a lighthouse and lit up the whole beach.

"Thank you. I bought it a couple of summers ago," Tical said modestly.

"Where did you come from? Mars?" Nautica said as she walked by his side.

Tical burst into laughter as he looked at her like she was crazy. "Mars? What you mean?"

"I mean, you seem like you got your life together. You're young, black, and doing good for yourself. You don't find a lot of dudes like you. Well, at least not where I'm from."

"Maybe, you need to find a new circle, because everybody I know lives like this."

Nautica giggled. She was waiting for Tical to smirk and chuckle, but when she saw no sign of it, she realized she'd met a major nigga and not a flake.

They reached his house and talked until the sun came up. No liquor, no sex, no drugs. Just deep conversation. For a brief couple of hours, Nautica forgot that she had no home or direction. Nautica had never experienced anything like that.

Tical fucked her that night. Not her body, but her mind. And she fell asleep fully clothed in his arms.

POLITICS AS USUAL

Chapter Fourteen

Tical sat across from Gunplay Murdock staring down at the chessboard. It was 10 a.m. and they were having breakfast together. Gunplay and Tical had a ritual. Every morning, over a game of chess, they would have conversations about their operation. Gunplay was Tical's enforcer, and you couldn't mention his name, if murder wasn't in the same sentence. He didn't get the name for nothing.

Only a few people knew of the magnitude of Tical's prominence in the streets. He had the city's heroin trade on lock, and chances were, if you were shooting dope in Baltimore, it came from him. He had a plug out of Florida that provided him with a high potency dope at dirt-cheap prices. His dope, which he labeled "primo," drove the market crazy.

"Yo, I heard some bullshit in the streets about that nigga Bear. Nigga talking slick out of his mouth. He been telling niggas that he's going to rock you," Gunplay said, not in an instigating way, but more out of concern.

Tical took his time before he spoke. The news didn't seem to affect him at all. "Gunplay, let me ask you a question. When have you ever known me to not stay two steps ahead of niggas? This game is like chess. I know that nigga is talking out the side of his neck, but I ain't worried. I'm already prepared for that. He a little nigga anyway."

"I already know, bruh. But the nigga talking like he trying to off you or something. Niggas is stepping out of line, fo' real. My lil niggas told me how he said you think you too big for niggas now. You know how niggas get when they see you doing your thing."

"Naw, it's cool. Let the nigga come. I got something for him. The nigga is just hot because I cut his ass off. He was on the east side with some stepped-on bullshit dope, selling it as primo, and giving my brand a bad name. I told that nigga to kill that shit, or I was going to cut him off. He kept doing the shit, so I stopped supplying him."

"So what you want me to do about this?"

"Just fall back. Let him come to me, and we will handle it then."

Although Tical was twenty-eight, he had sixteen years in the dope game. At his age most hustlers were either dead, in jail, or just getting in the game. But Tical was ready to retire. He was the walking blueprint of the perfect hustler.

Gunplay took his focus off the game. "Yo, what happened to shorty you left with last night?"

Tical smirked and glanced back to make sure Nautica wasn't around. Then he focused back on the chessboard and his next move. "Shorty upstairs 'sleep." He nodded his head in confirmation.

"Word? You bagged shorty that quick?"

"It ain't none of yo' business. But, naw, I ain't do nothing with her. She cool people, though. We just sat back and kicked it last night." Tical took a sip of the apple juice on the table.

"What do I look like, nigga? Boo-boo the fool? You mean to tell me she stayed the night in yo' bed and you ain't hit nothing?"

"Straight up. We ain't do nothing. She doesn't get down like that. She ain't like them hood rats around the way, ya dig? We just talked all night."

Nautica stood by the entrance eavesdropping on their conversation. She wore one of Tical's T-shirts that was way too big for her and hung down just above her knees. She'd heard their whole conversation and was surprised to find out that Tical was a drug dealer. The way he articulated himself and acted did not give out "hustler" in Nautica's mind. She was going to enter the kitchen, but she wanted to hear a little bit more before interrupting them.

"That's cool. Shorty was fine, though."

"Yeah, she bad as hell. I like her style. She got her shit together. I'm so used to stripper bitches and sack-chasers on me. It felt good to kick it with a levelheaded female for once."

"Yeah, you right. I saw that joint parked out front," Gunplay said, referring to Nautica's car. "That mu'fucka had to run her at least sixty stacks or more."

Tical nodded his head in agreement as he made another move on the chessboard.

Nautica knew at that moment that she wouldn't mention her past profession to Tical. She didn't want him to think less of her. She slowly walked around the corner, revealing herself. "Good morning," she said as she stared at Tical.

"Good morning," they both said in unison, slightly surprised by her presence.

Tical stood up and slightly grinned. He walked toward her. "How did you sleep?"

Nautica could smell his fresh scent as he stood over her. She looked at Tical and admired his body. He wore a wife-beater that hugged his physique, and baggy pants that still managed to display a small bulge in his midsection. And his butter Timberland only enticed her more. He was fresh to death.

"I slept fine. I see you get up early, huh." Nautica stood on her tippy toes to give him a peck on the cheek.

"Yeah, the early bird gets the worm. You remember my man from last night, right?" Tical said as he looked back at Murdock.

"Yeah, it was Gunplay, right?" Nautica waved quickly. She couldn't forget a crazy name like that.

"Yeah. What's good, shorty?" Gunplay stood up and finished the last of his apple juice. "Yo, I'ma take off." He gave Tical a pound. "It was good seeing you again," he said to Nautica, and just like that he was gone.

Nautica hopped on the counter and swung her legs childishly. Tical focused his attention back on her, staring at her and running his fingers through her hair.

Nautica closed her eyes and enjoyed the sensation of his strong hand sifting through her hair. She kissed the palm of his hand and then stared into his warm hazel eyes. "So, you never gave me a tour of your house." She hopped off the counter and circled the marble countertop that sat in the middle of the spacious area, admiring the white marble floors and flawless area that he called his kitchen.

"I got you. Follow me." Tical began to walk toward a small set of steps that led to a den next to the kitchen.

As soon as Nautica entered the area she was in awe. The oak wood theme gave the room a dark setting, and the brown leather couches matched the shelves perfectly. The walls were lined with books. In fact, his collection of over four hundred books resembled a small library. A large bearskin rug lay in the middle of the floor.

Tical walked over to his large handcrafted wooden desk that sat at the back of the room. "This is my study. I do a lot of thinking in here."

"Very nice. I'm impressed." Nautica began to run her fingers over the books in his bookshelf.

"Thanks." Tical motioned for Nautica to follow him upstairs. "This is the first guestroom."

She peeked inside the fully furnished room. The spacious room looked like a master bedroom. "One of your guest-rooms? How many rooms do you have?"

"Six," Tical said in a humble tone.

Nautica went past a room with a note on the door that read *do not enter* in bubble crayon letters. It seemed like a teenager wrote it. She grabbed the back of Tical's wifebeater, as she stopped. "Whose room is this?"

"Oh, that's Millie's room."

Tical pushed the door open. The room was draped in cream and brown and had a plasma TV mounted on the wall. Nautica recognized immediately the feminine touch in the decor. The floor had all-white carpet, and a queen-sized bed sat in the middle of the spacious room.

"Who is Millie?" Nautica tried her best not to sound too eager to find out who the girl was.

Nautica and Tical walked into the room. Nautica picked up a framed picture from the nightstand and studied it. The picture was of Tical and another girl that wasn't much younger than him on it. They were at a club, standing in front of an airbrushed background, both holding up bottles of Moët, and Tical had his arm around her, not in a companion way, but like a man would throw an arm around his nigga.

Tical watched Nautica observe the picture. "Millie is like my li'l sister. That was her eighteenth birthday party I threw for her at the club."

Nautica didn't want to be walking through another woman's house and get herself into some bullshit. "Like your little sister?"

"Nah, nah, it ain't even like that. I been looking after her since she was young." Tical walked behind Nautica and rested his hands on her thighs.

Nautica stared at the slim, chocolate girl on the picture. She kind of resembled Lauryn Hill, with her full, dark lips and flawless smile. "She's pretty. So, she lives here with you?"

"No, she just has a room here. She got her own spot about a year ago, and I just never changed the room, you know."

Nautica put down the picture and followed Tical down the stairs and back into the kitchen, where he pulled out a chair for her and waved for her to come sit down. She smiled, accepting his invitation.

Tical then walked over to the refrigerator and began to pull out food. "You eat eggs and bacon, right?" he asked as he washed his hands.

"Yeah. You're going to cook for me?" Nautica had never had a man prepare a meal for her.

He calmly nodded his head as he began to break up the eggs.

Nautica couldn't stop smiling. Tical was looking sexy as ever, and he made her feel like a princess that morning, catering to her like he was a chef serving royalty.

Just as they were finishing up their breakfast, Tical received a call on his cell phone. He didn't say much to the person on the other end. He hung up and said, "I'm sorry, ma. We're going to have to finish this a little later."

Tical walked around the table and grabbed Nautica from behind. When she felt his package on the small of her back, the hair on the back of her neck stood on end.

She turned around and looked into his dreamy eyes. "That's fine. I had a great time with you last night, Tical." She smiled. "Thank you." She wiped her hands with a napkin.

Tical bent down and kissed the top of her head. "The pleasure was all mine."

"What are your plans for tonight?"

"Not much.' Nautica said as she stood up and stood face to face with him.

"Well, I have a luxury box at the Baltimore Ravens game. Do you like football?" he asked, returning her gaze.

"I love football," Nautica lied.

"How does eight o'clock sound?"

"Great!" she said, her tone similar to that of an eager five-year-old.

Tical was completely turned on by Nautica. He ran his fingers through her hair and laid the softest kiss on her forehead. "Okay, I will call you later to arrange for a car to pick you up. Sorry I had to end this so abruptly, but I have to handle something very important." Tical headed toward his den. "I'll call you for your address later," he said before disappearing into the darkness of the other room.

He obviously had something important to take care of, which only made him even more attractive to Nautica. She loved his style. He was so hood, yet so businesslike. She smiled as she went upstairs to get her things.

Bear's all-black, dark-tint Lincoln Navigator was parked a couple of houses down from Tical's home. He leaned back and observed patiently as he sorted out the plan in his mind to get at Tical. He watched a woman trot across the sands and head toward her car that sat a couple hundred yards from the back entrance.

Bear smirked, knowing that he'd finally caught Tical slipping. He fantasized about being at the top of the totem pole in the streets of Baltimore as the head dopeman. Tical was the only person in his way. He couldn't compete with Tical. Every time he dropped his heroin price, Tical would lower his. Bear was forced to cop his work from Tical and become one of his workers. And Bear wasn't going for that.

"I'm a boss," he whispered to himself as he looked down at his lap and watched the woman's head go up and down on his shaft. He put his hand on the back of her head and made her swallow him whole as he released himself in the back of her throat.

Bear's six foot four, 280-pound frame led to his nickname, which suited him perfectly. He shifted position in the seat to pull up his pants, sliding his rod back into confinement. He wiped the sweat from his eyebrow and then rubbed his full beard, brushing it downward.

He sat back and watched his chocolate beauty use the mirror in the visor to straighten up her hair and re-apply her lipstick. "You the best, Lola. You know that, girl?" he said, admiring her ebony skin and Indian-textured hair.

"Nigga, I know."

There to handle business with Tical, Lola's beauty had Bear wanting to pop off before going in for the kill. He'd brought her along because she was the one who'd tipped him off about Tical's home. He'd been trying to find out where Tical lived for weeks, and when he met her at the club a week earlier, she'd mentioned that she used to talk to one of Tical's street generals. A light bulb flicked on inside of his head then. He knew Lola would be of great use to him.

After Lola told Bear that she rode over to Tical's house one time with the general and knew exactly where he lay his head, and that he didn't have any security at his main home because no one knew about it but his closest confidantes, he began spending time with her, just so he could squeeze more information out of her.

He made sure not to let Lola see too much. She'd told him about Tical's business within their first hour of talking, so he knew she had loose lips. He'd never had sex with her, but her head game was crazy. So he showed his appreciation by cashing her out many times in just that short time that they'd met.

Excited about the thought of knocking Tical off, Bear had promised Lola a trip to Hawaii. That's why he had a bag full of money and two round-trip plane trips in the back of his truck. So they'd be thousands of feet in the air, drinking bubbly, and on their way to the island right after he took care of business. His only regret, though, was forgetting his "lucky" pistol, a gold-plated 9 mm with his initials engraved on it.

"All right, you ready?" Bear cocked his gun back and took another look at Tical's home.

"Are you sure he's in there?" Lola popped her gum loudly and ghetto.

"Yeah, I just saw him walk to the door. He's in there for sure." Bear kept his eyes on the place.

The plan was for Lola to walk to the door and ask Tical, could she use his phone because her car had broke down nearby, and when he let her in, she would pull the gun on him. Then Bear would come in and take over from there. He needed Lola to get him through the door.

Bear felt warm inside, thinking he had manipulated her mind so quick, and her being so beautiful only boosted his already gigantic ego.

"Okay, you still got that gun I gave you, right?"

"Yeah, I got it right here." Lola reached into her purse and pulled out the small-caliber gun.

"Cool, cool. Look, ring the doorbell, and when he answer, you do what I told you to do. Once you get in, peep his spot. If he ain't strapped and alone, pull yo' shit out and then call me. I'ma be right outside, ready to come in, baby. After I get in, you can come out and wait for me in the car." Bear reached over and gave Lola a peck on the cheek.

"I got you, daddy." Lola hopped out of the truck and pulled down her skirt, which was riding her.

Just as she reached the driveway, heading toward the house, Bear peeped his rearview mirror and saw the delivery man walking on the sidewalk and onto Tical's property with a package in his hand, which meant he was about to knock on Tical's door and mess up plans. Bear had to think quick. He rolled down his window and called for the man, while Lola walked up the driveway toward the front door. She didn't even notice the mailman walking a few feet behind her.

Bear stuck his head out of the window. "Yo! I'm right here."

The mailman did a 180 and began walking to the truck. Oh, hello, Mr. Manny. I need you to sign off for the package."

The mailman had his hat pulled down tight and didn't even look up. He was looking at the package to make sure he had the right address. As he pat his pockets in search for a pen, Bear held out his hand for the package.

The delivery man looked up, displaying his face. It was Gunplay disguised as a UPS worker. He dropped the box and pressed his chrome .45-pistol to Bear's neck. "Surprise, mu'fucka!"

Tical sat back behind his red oak desk in his oversized leather office chair taking deep puffs of his Kush weed. He inhaled, held his head back, and slowly blew smoke circles into the air, thinking about the phone call he'd just received from Gunplay Murdock. He knew that Bear would eventually jump stupid and fall right into his trap. He heard noises coming from the front room and immediately knew who it was.

Moments later Gunplay, Bear, and a woman entered the room, joining him. Bear had his hands in the air as Gunplay dug his gun into

Bear's neck directing him to the chair that sat directly in front of Tical.

The woman walked over to Tical and pecked him on the cheek. "Hey, Tical." She shot a hateful stare at Bear.

"What up, Millie? You good?" Tical gave her a welcoming smile. He then focused his attention back on Bear, who looked like he'd seen a ghost.

"Yeah, I'm good now. This bitch-ass nigga is disgusting. I don't know how much longer I could've fronted like I was feeling this clown." Millie wanted to spit, thinking about what she had to do to gain Bear's trust.

Millie was a down-ass bitch. She'd swallowed the enemy's cum for her team, which was totally out of her character, but she did it for the good of her team. She reduced herself to a groupie whore just to get close to Bear. She would never tell Tical that she hit him off in the car, but she did what she had to do to hold down her part.

"You dirty-ass bitch!" Bear barked, his head cocked to the side because Gunplay dug the barrel into his temple.

Gunplay whacked Bear in the back of the head with his pistol. "Watch ya mouth." He sat in the chair next to him, gun still pointed at Bear's head.

Tical sat back relaxed and calm as he and Millie chuckled at the look on Bear's face. Bear was totally floored. He thought he was plotting on Tical, but he was the one getting plotted on. Tical took his time putting the blunt out and folded both of his hands together. He stared intently at Bear. "Why, Bear? Why, nigga? I let you eat!" Tical said, more intense with every word, but his tone still low. He couldn't understand how Bear let his pride get in the way of making paper. "You're in this shit for the wrong reason, fam. You couldn't stand the fact that"— Tical picked up the bottle of Hennessy, poured a small amount into a glass, and took the shot effortlessly—"you're not me." He released a menacing smile and sat the glass on his coaster.

"Man, it—"

Tical placed his index finger on his lip. "Shh," cutting Bear off. Tical stared into Bear's eyes. "You know what the problem is? There are too many chiefs, not enough Indians. The only thing you had to do was to play your position and get rich. But you didn't want that, you wanted this." Tical opened his hands toward Bear.

"What was I supposed to do? Huh? You was telling me how to cut my dope and trying to tell me how to run my business."

"Nigga, it wasn't yo' dope. It was my product! Nigga, you worked for me, if you wanted to or not. You got to stepping on the dope, making it not worth shit, throwing dirt on my name. Matter of fact, why am I'm explaining to this nigga."

Tical grabbed the remote that sat on his desk and turned on the surround sound CD player, pumping the sounds of Jay-Z's "Can I Live" throughout the room. Everyone began to slowly bob their head to the melodic violins serenading the room, except for Bear.

Tical closed his eyes and enjoyed the street classic. He thought about how much the song closely reflected his life in the streets.

Bear grew a confused look on his face when he saw them bobbing their heads. Little did he know, Tical didn't turn the music up loud to enjoy the song, he did it so the neighbors wouldn't hear the gunshot blast that was only seconds away.

"Gunplay, show 'em what you got." Tical got up from his chair and walked away, and Millie followed close behind.

When the loud blast echoed through the house, neither Millie nor Tical flinched a muscle. They knew Gunplay had rocked him to sleep with a slug to the face. *Boom!*

REAL BITCHES DO REAL THINGS: MEET MILLIE

Chapter Fifteen

Millian, aka Millie, flopped on her bed and stared at the ceiling. She was glad the little charade was over and that Bear was finally gone. She hated pretending that she had interest in him. She'd heard that Bear was talking slick about Tical, and she volunteered to approach him. At first Tical rejected the idea, being overprotective of Millie and all, but after a week, she'd persuaded him to see things her way. She understood that Bear wasn't easy to touch, but she knew the fastest way to a man is in between his legs.

Millie promised that she wouldn't sleep with Bear, just tease him until the right time. She felt that it would be the smarter approach, rather than Tical sending his soldiers to kill Bear and risk taking loses. But Bear was a street nigga just as well as Tical, so Millie knew she had to be extra cautious. Her method worked like a charm.

"That nigga was so irritating," she said referring to Bear. She sat up and looked around the room that she used to call home. Tical had left it just the way it was, not moving or touching anything. She missed staying there because she always felt safe with him.

She picked up the picture with Tical and herself that sat on her nightstand and smiled, looking at the only man she'd ever loved. She secretly was in love with Tical and admired everything about him. Tical had never looked at her like more than a little sister, but she frequently dreamed about being his woman. "I love you, Tical," she whispered as she studied the pictures.

Tical appeared in the doorway. "I love you too, lil sis."

Millie heard his low, raspy voice. She smiled and quickly put away the picture. "Boy, you better stop running up on me like you crazy. You scared me. I could have popped you." She scooted over so he could sit next to her.

"Pop me? With what? You ain't even strapped. You got your little hot girl outfit on," Tical pulled at her skimpy halter top. He wasn't used to seeing her in sexy clothing. She was more of a down dresser, staying fresh in the latest gear, but she wasn't into skirts or dresses. Usually she'd be sporting the newest tight-fitting velour hookup or nice-looking jogging suits.

Millie reached under her skirt and pulled out the small .22 Tical had purchased for her for her eighteenth birthday. "I keep one, fam. You didn't know."

They both laughed.

"You crazy. You know that?"

Tical observed the young lady he'd molded since she was fifteen. Only eight years her senior, he had witnessed her grow from a girl to a woman over the past five years.

"Well, you taught me to keep one on me at all times, so just because I'm wearing this bullshit doesn't mean I don't stick to the script." She walked over to her closet and pulled off her shirt, only having on a bra.

Tical didn't look, out of respect, and had no desire to. "Thanks for doing that, though. That was some real shit you did." He looked at the missed calls on his phone.

"Stop playing, Tical. You know I'm down for the team. I just had to put work in, ya know," she said as she slid on a small Roca wear T-shirt.

"No doubt." Tical nodded his head up and down.

"So you want to go the bar and watch the game tonight? Ravens are going to whoop the Packers ass." Millie slid her pants on under her skirt before finally taking her skirt off. She kept her eyes on Tical, hoping he would look, but he never did. He always was respectful to her, and that's why she loved him so much.

She glanced at the tattoo in small cursive letters right above her breast—T-I-C-A-L. She had gotten it without him knowing. She would never tell him about it, because she didn't get it for him, she got it for herself, to remind her how much he'd done for her, and changed her life for the better. She would be forever loyal to him.

"Not this week, Millie. I'm going to the luxury box tonight. You should come," Tical said, his attention on his phone.

Millie was kind of disappointed, but she didn't let it show. They would always watch the game with each other on Sunday. Being around Tical and Gunplay so much, she became a devoted football fan also.

"Oh, okay. You got a business meeting or something?".

"Naw, I'm taking a friend up to the box. Just to chill." Tical watched as Millie brushed her hair in the mirror into a tight ponytail pulled straight back. Her back was turned toward him.

He glanced at her plump ass and slender figure. *Damn! Millie growing up.* She was slim, dark, and was attractive to many men. But he couldn't see himself looking at her in that light and quickly erased the notion out of his mind. He focused his eyes on hers through the mirror.

"A friend? So you must be feeling this friend, huh?"

"She's cool. It ain't nothing like that. We just are going to hang out." Tical rubbed his facial hair. "What happened to you and ol' boy?"

"Oh, you talking about Banks? That nigga was a lame. I had to let him go. I hate a nigga that suffocate you. He had a problem with me getting money out here too. He couldn't stand that I had more clout in the streets than him."

Millie plopped on the bed next to Tical. She really left the guy because in her eyes no one else compared to Tical. No matter who she dated, they never could stimulate her mind and make her feel the way he did. She always said if she fell in love, it would be with a man just like Tical. She had to get a replica, because she knew she never could have Tical.

"Well, you know how dominant you are." Tical stood up. "You probably was rubbing it all in his face, trying to be boss."

"I am boss, nigga." Millie grinned.

"Yeah, yeah, I know," Tical said sarcastically. "Yo, I'm about to call the cleaners to clean up the mess, but are we still on for Friday right?" The "cleaners" was a nickname for the funeral home workers he had on payroll to dispose of the dead bodies his team created.

"Yep, wouldn't miss it for anything," Millie said, referring to the Friday brunches they'd been having for five years straight. No matter how far away they were from each other, they never missed that meeting. When she was fifteen, Tical promised her that Friday would always be theirs and he hadn't broken that promise to her yet.

Millie watched as Tical faded into the darkness of the hallway, and she smiled, totally in love with his swagger. She lay on the bed and thought about when they first met. He was the first person to ever show any love for her. She owed her life to him.

Five years earlier

"Yeah, you black bitch. Squeeze my ass." The overweight white trucker pounded the young girl who lay on this cot in the back of his truck.

Millie closed her eyes and moaned, pretending to enjoy the small red penis that went in and out of her. *He needs to hurry up.* She momentarily opened her eyes and saw the man's mouth wide open and drool threatening to fall. She gripped his sweaty butt, and he began to pump faster and faster, until he finally exploded into the condom. He grunted and gave her one last deep thrust before rolling off.

Millie quickly sat up and began to put on her clothes, which were on the side of the cot. She wanted to get out of the smelly truck, so she could get back to her post and make more money. Fully clothed, she looked at the man, who panted heavily and stared into space as if he was in a dream.

"Run it, big daddy," she demanded in her heavy New York accent. She held out her hand and began moving her fingers, signaling for him to pay up.

He reached into his boot and pulled out a wad of money. He peeled off a fifty-dollar bill and tossed it to her. "There you go, Sunshine," he said, as he stuffed his money back into his boot.

"Thanks, honey." Millie smiled. She rubbed the man's limp penis and stood up, straightening up her clothes and licking her lips sexily. She put the fifty into her purse and closed it. "So when am I'm going to see you again, baby? You got some good dick."

The man, still on his back and naked, stared at her and smiled. "Well, I have to drop off a shipment to North Carolina, and I should be heading back this way in a week or so." He sat up and slipped on his grungy white briefs.

"Well, I'll be right here waiting for you, big boy," she said, egging him on.

"You're always at this truck stop?" He thought about getting another shot of the sweet thing he'd just pounded. The truckstop was in a huge parking lot that also had a diner that truckers from all around the country frequented.

"Yep, just about every day. I'll be waiting for you, too. It's hard to find a good fuck in this business, ya know." Millie watched him eat up every word. "Well, I'm about to get out of here. You have a safe trip, and make sure you stop and see me on your way back." She began to walk backwards to the front cab of the truck. She tripped and fell over his big boots that sat in the middle of the floor.

"Are you okay?"

"Whew! Yeah, I'm okay." Millie, an embarrassed look on her face, scrambled to pick up her purse. She moved the boots out of her way and got back up. "That was humiliating." She smugly smiled and then headed out. "Come back and see me now!"

"I sure will, honey."

Millie stepped out of the truck and hurried to the rest stop. She looked down at the wad of money in her hands that she'd just lifted from his boots.

She flipped through the bills as she walked briskly toward the diner just a few hundred feet from her. "Hell yeah, this looks about five hundred dollars." She kept looking back at the truck, hoping she would have time to get away before he discovered he'd just been robbed.

Although Millie was only fifteen, she had the wits and savvy of a full-grown woman. Just looking at her, no one would guess that she was underage. Her body was plump in all the right places, and she conducted herself like a seasoned veteran.

She'd been working the streets for her pimp stepfather ever since she started to grow breasts. Her mother's husband had been in the pimping game for years. Millie's mother had overdosed when she was only twelve. She quickly began to see her stepfather's true colors after her mother passed. It didn't take long for him to introduce her to the family business.

Close to the diner now, she looked back one more time to make sure he wasn't coming for her and that the coast was clear. Once she didn't see him, she pushed open the doors and took a deep breath. The only thing on her mind was copping a fix with the dealer posted in the back of the diner. But she only had a few minutes before her stepfather would come to check up on her. She also had to worry about the trucker finding out what she'd done and coming for her.

Millie's stepfather had introduced her to heroin just months before. She loved the warm sensation of the drug crawling up her vein and giving her a dope fiend lean, and it seemed like her pain went away when she was high off the drug. When the magic of the drug entered her veins it made her feel invincible and without a care in the world. Just the way she thought life should be.

She saw the dark-skinned guy with a baseball cap on sitting in the back of the diner, as he always did. She hurried over to him and peeled off a twenty from the wad she'd just lifted. She sat across from him as he casually read a newspaper. She cleared her throat to get his attention.

"How much?" he said, his eyes still on the paper.

She looked at the door. "A twenty pack."

"You know you're too young to be fucking with this shit?" He shook his head from side to side.

"Nigga, quit with the bullshit. You want this money or not?" Millie thought he was picking the wrong time to contest her drug habit, especially since she had copped from him dozens of times. "So, nigga, do you?" She pushed the twenty toward him.

The man looked up and scanned the room. He folded his newspaper and sat it on top of the money. He discreetly picked up the money from under the paper and stuffed it in his pocket. He then put his hands on his lap, as did Millie, and gave her the small baggie under the table.

Millie smiled and headed out the back door and into the porta-potty that sat in the back of the place, her get-high spot.

Tical scanned the parking lot as he sat in a black S-10 pickup truck. He tried his best to look like a farmer with his bucket fishing hat and plaid shirt. He glanced at his clock and sucked his teeth. "Where this dude at?"

Tical had $60,000 dollars in the bag next to him to buy three kilos of coke and had been waiting for thirty minutes for his connect. He had laced the piles of haystacks in the back bed of the truck with pepper, to throw off police dogs, and had planned on stuffing the coke into pre-cut compartments in the haystacks, so he could return back to B-more undetected.

"That's why I don't like fucking with this New York nigga," he said to himself. He saw a young dark-skinned girl hurry past his car and into the diner. He was just about ready to leave when he saw his man Red pull up in a red Lexus with black tint. "This nigga stupid!" He hated that Red had the audacity to bring a flashy car to their exchange and regretted doing business with him.

As Red parked the car, Tical peeped his surroundings. He grabbed the bag and stepped out of the car, headed over to Red. Just then, he saw a heavyset man with just some tight white underwear on attire yelling obscenities as he stepped out of his eighteen-wheeler. The man's eyes danced around the parking lot.

Tical quickly focused his attention back on Red's car as he approached it. He opened the door, and the loud sounds of Tupac blasted from the speakers. He quickly turned the volume down.

Red extended his hand for a shake. "What's up, Baltimore?"

"Man, you got the shit?" Tical left Red's hands hanging in the air.

"Man, what's wrong with you today?"

"Nothing." Tical asked again, "So where the shit?"

Red reached in his back seat for a bookbag and sat it on his lap. "I got you together right here. You got the cash?"

Tical and Red exchanged bags, and both of them looked at the contents of their bag. Tical dipped his pinky in the Ziploc bag and ran it across his gums. Moments later, his gums began to numb. Red had hit him with some good product once again. "I'm out," Tical said, as Red thumbed through the money.

"So quick?" Red asked, his eyes on the money.

Tical opened the door and got out. He stooped and looked at Red. "Let me say this, and I'm only going to say it once, you stupid mu'fucka—Never drive this car when you dealing with me on business. You moving like you an amateur or something." He slammed the door, not giving Red a chance to respond, and headed into the diner to use the bathroom.

Red wanted to put Tical in his place, but it was something about Tical's eyes that made him think twice about jumping stupid. He couldn't understand how a guy so young acted like he was the man in charge.

Tical wasn't big at that time, but all that would change in the future. He was going to eventually switch the game and deal heroin, and become a legend on Baltimore streets.

Millie nodded off in the porta-potty, drool sliding down her lip. She yanked her head back when she felt her chin touch her chest. She opened her eyes and looked around the stall, trying to remember where she was at. The smell of urine almost made her gag. She positioned herself upright, the needle still stuck in her arm. She eased the needle from her skin and placed it in her purse, opened the door, and stepped out.

She smiled as the air hit her face. It felt good to her, and the air tickled her skin. The heroin put her in a place only junkies could fathom. Millie had no idea how long she had nodded in the port-a-potty. She was hoping her stepfather didn't roll up on her post while she was in the stall, because she didn't want to hear his mouth when she got home.

She walked around the building, preparing to get back on her post. At that point she'd forgotten that she'd stolen nearly five hundred dollars from her last john. She looked around the parking lot for potential customers. Her legs wobbled as she caught a nod while walking, almost falling. She almost got hit by a red Lexus exiting the lot, the driver blasting his horn at her.

She stuck up her middle finger and continued to walk as she began to head toward the area the truckers usually parked. Millie held her head down as she walked uncoordinatedly.

"You dirty bitch," a white man screamed, shotgun in hand. He raised his gun and pointed it at her

"Aw fuck!" Millie made a dash for the row of cars a few feet away from her and ducked down. *Aw shit! Aw shit!* She crouched down and maneuvered through the rows of cars, trying to shake the ranting man.

"Where you at, li'l black bitch?" He looked around crazily, going in and out of rows.

Millie heard the man's voice getting closer and closer.

She had to think fast. She hopped into the bed of a small truck nearby and laid on her back, positioning herself tightly in between the two big haystacks sat in the back.

After a couple of minutes laying there, she began to nod and fell into a deep sleep. She didn't even feel someone get in the car and pull off.

Tical glanced at the bag with the coke and smiled as he rode down the highway. He wanted to put the coke into the haystacks, but when he came out of the diner and saw a crazy-ass white man toting a gun and yelling, he decided to get out of the area before the cops came. "Mu'fucka crazy," he said to himself.

After driving about thirty miles down the highway heading back to Baltimore, Tical saw a sign indicating that a rest stop was three miles ahead. He'd put the coke in the stash spot then. He pulled his truck onto the next exit and spotted a small gas station just off the ramp. He drove up to the station, got out, and quickly tossed the bag in the back. He then headed into the store to pay for some gas before he hid the coke in the haystacks.

Millie jumped up when something hit her in the face. She couldn't remember where she was at, one of the effects of heroin. She saw the haystacks surrounding her, and then it hit her. She'd been hiding from the john. Her heart began to pump quickly. She looked at the unfamiliar setting. "Where the fuck am I?" She began to take the hay out of her hair. She looked at the bookbag that hit her in the face and wondered who'd tossed it. She realized that she'd nodded while hiding in the back of the truck. *Fuck!* She had no idea how far she was from the truck stop. *Am I even still in New York?*

As she stepped out of the truck with the bag in her hand, she heard a gun click and quickly turned around.

"Li'l ma, I don't know who you are, but you barked up the wrong tree," a calm, raspy voice said to her. The man pointed his gun at her chest. "Red sent you, huh?" He yanked the bag from her.

He lowered his gun and quickly grabbed Millie by the arm and checked her for a gun with his other hand.

Tical had seen her rise from the back of his truck while he was paying for gas. He thought Red had sent her to rob him for the same product he'd just bought, an old stick-up kid trick.

"You got five seconds to tell me who sent you, or I'ma send one of these slugs through your stomach. Try me!" Tical said, meaning every single word. He noticed how young the girl was and slightly loosened his grip on her.

Millie was terrified, and it showed through her youthful eyes. "I'm sorry, sir. I just hid in the back of your truck because this crazy mu'fucka was after me. I swear to God!" She began to tear up, knowing she was about to die.

Tical thought about the man screaming in the parking lot. "What he look like?" he asked, his tone cold.

"He was a white trucker-looking mu'fucka." Millie, her hands still in the air, kept her eyes on Tical's gun.

Tical realized she could be telling the truth, but he still remained cautious. He stared at her for a second and then decided to ease up. "Get in the car." He put his gun back into his waist and looked around to make sure no one was watching.

Millie turned, shaking like crazy, and headed toward the vehicle. She thought about making a dash for it, but she didn't want to get shot in the back. *What the fuck have I gotten myself in to? This farmer-looking mu'fucka about to take me somewhere and rape and kill me.*

"And put yo' hands down." Tical took one last look around the gas station. He put the coke in the hidden compartments in the haystacks, while keeping an eye on Millie through the back window.

Once he finished, Tical sat in the car and remained silent, wondering if her story was legit. The tears forming in her eyes and her jitteriness displayed her terror. He didn't think she'd cause him any harm. He stuck his gun in his waist for easy access. "Look, I'm not going to hurt you, so relax. I will take you back to the truck stop, okay," he said in a soothing tone, trying not to scare the girl anymore than she already was.

Millie nodded her head, but she still didn't know his real intentions.

Tical started up the truck and prepared to go fifty miles back to drop her back off at her post. They rode in silence as Tical kept his eyes on the road.

Millie was the first to speak. "So where are you from? I can tell that you're not from around here," she said, beginning to feel a tad bit more comfortable.

Tical didn't even look at her. He had a bad feeling about the girl and couldn't help feel that he was being set up. He frowned up. "Chill out with the small talk, ma. I ain't got any convo for you."

"Dang, I was just trying to be polite." Millie began to scratch her arms. Her high had fallen, and she began to get the itch that most fiends got after they got high. She felt like an army of small ants were marching up and down her veins.

Tical glanced at Millie's arm and saw the needle marks. He looked at her gestures and knew she was a user. He began to feel bad about being so rude to her and forced himself to talk to her. "How old are you?"

After a few seconds of silence, Millie noticed that Tical was glancing down at her marks. He continued after not getting a response.

"Well, you don't look a day over sixteen, and you out here bad. That shit ain't for you." He shook his head in disbelief. *They getting younger and younger,* he thought, switching lanes.

"How do you know what's for me? I'm a grown-ass woman," Millie said, snapping her neck back and forth.

"Grown-ass woman, huh?"

Millie might've fooled a lot of people, but not Tical. He knew she was a minor. Although she had a developed body, she didn't have the gestures of a person who'd been through life yet. "You can't be any older than sixteen or seventeen, but whatever you say." He looked at the chocolate girl that sat next to him, and felt drawn to her. Maybe it was because she resembled his mother, with her skin tone and big, dark brown eyes.

Just then, the flashing lights of a police car shined.

Tical glanced in his rearview mirror. "Fuck!" He pulled over to the side of the road, big butterflies in his stomach. He reached into his waist and discreetly slid his gun to the side of his seat. He had a life sentence hidden in his haystacks and had already made up his mind to go out blasting if the cop asked him to step out.

Millie watched Tical become noticeably shaken up as he slid the gun to the side and click off the safety.

The cop got out of his cruiser and approached the truck.

Tical, knowing the drill, kept his hand on the steering wheel. "Good evening, sir."

"License and registration," the cop said, his hand near his gun.

"No problem." Tical reached over Millie's lap and into the glove box. After retrieving his papers, he handed it to the officer.

The officer took the papers and looked suspiciously at the haystacks in the back. He went to his cruiser. He ran Tical's name and found out he had a previous gun charge. He went back to the truck. "Who is the young lady with you?" he asked, glancing over at her.

"That's my younger sister—"

"Millie!"

"Is that right?" The officer walked to the back of the truck. "What's the haystacks for?" He began to take a closer look at them.

When Tical turned slightly to look back at the cop, his gun slid off his lap and onto the side of the seat. "Damn!" he said in a low tone.

The officer heard a clink and quickly turned around. He approached the window. "What's that, boy?" he asked, his hand on his gun.

Tical tensed up. "Nothing, sir."

"Step out of the car, please," the officer said, keeping a close eye on him.

Tical stepped out of the car slowly. He knew he had to stay calm.

The officer escorted him to the rear of the truck and told him to turn around.

Fuck! Tical watched helplessly as the officer made Millie stand at the rear of the car while he searched it.

After a couple minutes, the cop made Millie get back in the car. He told Tical, "I'm going to let you off with a warning."

Tical was relieved. He could tell the cop was disappointed not to find anything. When he got back into the car and looked down at the floor, he didn't see the gun. Millie must've hidden it from the cop. He took a deep breath and pulled off, knowing he had just dodged a bullet. "Thanks." He glanced over at Millie.

"It ain't nothing." Millie reached into her pantyhose and pulled out the gun. She placed it on Tical's lap.

Tical lightened up, appreciative of her quick thinking. "So what's your name again?"

"Millian, but everyone calls me Millie."

"You're pretty sharp, I see."

"Yeah, I have to be," Millie said, scratching her arms and drawing blood. "The streets tend to keep you on your shit."

"Who got you started?"

"Started on what?"

Tical gave her a look that said, "Don't insult my intelligence." He looked down at her arm and nodded his head in its direction.

"My stepfather."

"Your stepfather? That's fucked up." Tical shook his head from side to side.

Millie studied Tical's gestures and mannerisms and immediately was attracted. Even though he had on farmer clothes, she knew that wasn't his style. The way he talked and took his time with every syllable had Millie wanting to learn more about the older man. Her mind was trained to look at every man as a potential john.

She unbuckled her seatbelt and took the gum out of her mouth. She then leaned over the seat and attempted to put her head on Tical's crotch, but he gently pushed her away.

Tical frowned up and looked at her like she was insane. "Fall back, ma. It ain't that type of party."

Millie grew self-conscious about her looks. She got teased in school about her dark skin tone and had internalized the notion, the lighter, the prettier. "What's wrong? You don't think I'm pretty?"

"Actually, I think you're beautiful, but I ain't trying to take it there with you. You're way too young for me," Tical said, sensing her insecurity.

"You really think I'm pretty?" Millie ran her fingers through her damaged hair. She wasn't used to anybody telling her how beautiful she was unless they wanted to have sex with her.

"I wouldn't say it if I didn't mean it."

Tical wanted to change the subject, so he began to ask her common questions, and they talked all the way until they reached the truck stop.

The hour ride only seemed like minutes to Millie, who had fallen in love with Tical's swagger in the thirty miles they traveled on the highway. When he pulled up to the stop, she saw her stepfather waiting outside of the diner with a small bottle of Five O'clock gin in his hand. Millie's heart began to pump, because whenever he drank, he would beat and sexually abuse her.

Tical put his truck in park and hit the unlock button. "Okay, here's your stop." He looked over at Millie and noticed her discomfort. He followed her eyes and saw her staring at the man sanding in front of the diner. "That's your stepfather, huh?"

Millie nodded her head and became teary eyed as she thought about the night ahead of her.

Tical looked at Millie then back at her stepfather. He couldn't release her to the wolves after what she'd done for him. "I'll be right back." He grabbed his gun, put it in his waist, and jumped out of the car, headed toward the man.

Millie's stepfather leaned against the building, smoking a cigarette. He'd been looking for Millie for the past thirty minutes and didn't notice Tical walk up on him.

Tical grabbed him by his collar and slammed him up against the wall. "Yo, man, what's yo' damn problem." He looked deep into the man's eyes, as he kept a tight grip on him. Though full of rage, Tical kept his voice calm and clear. "Yo, is that your daughter in that car right there?" He threw his head in the direction of Millie, who sat in his passenger side.

Confused, the man squinted as he looked inside the car. "Oh, I see what you getting to," he said, growing relaxed. "She's a hot commodity around here. Tell you what, give me fifty and you can have her all night. Believe me, she's good. I've tested the goods myself." He puffed his cigarette.

Thoughts of Tical's own mother being killed by an abusive boyfriend when he was only sixteen came back to him. Millie resembled his mother so much, he instantly felt connected to her. Tical wrapped his strong hand around the man's neck and squeezed as tight as he could.

The man struggled for air and dug his nails into Tical's hand, trying to get him to release him.

"You are a bitch-ass nigga. You feeding that li'l girl poison and killing her slowly. She's not even old enough to understand what she's doing to her body. I should put a hole through yo' mu'fuckin' dome. Niggas like you make me sick. You can't get out here and hustle for yours, so you leech off of the weak. But you the weak one!"

Tical grabbed his pistol from his waist and put the barrel in the man's mouth. When the man looked like he was about to lose consciousness, he released his hold and watched the man fall to his knees, gasping for air. Breathing heavily now, Tical turned around and walked toward his truck.

Millie was confused, not knowing what Tical was going to do to her. She didn't hear any of the exchange, she just saw Tical grab her stepfather by the neck.

The car was silent, except for Tical's heaving breathing.

After Tical gathered himself, he said to Millie, "You're coming with me, okay?" He stared at her with his piercing hazel eyes.

Something came over Millie, and in a situation where another girl would've been scared, she became comfortable. She slowly nodded her head in agreement. Tears formed in her eyes. Not tears of pain, but of joy. She knew that, from that day on, she would be okay.

Tical took Millie under his wing and taught her everything he knew, as he would a younger sister. He helped her kick her heroin habit cold turkey and told her that he would kill her before letting her go down that road again. He also made her return to school.

Tical had always told Millie that her living with him would just be temporary, but weeks turned into months, and months into years. They had become family. After three years of grooming, and on her eighteenth birthday, he introduced Millie to the hustle game, and she took to it like a duck to water. Most people said she was the female version of Tical, and rightfully so. Tical had promised her that, no matter what, they would always be family. That's why he made Friday their day to bond and talk. Even after she moved out, he wanted to keep the ritual going. He never told her, but he wanted to make sure that she never messed with drugs again, and that was his slick way of keeping her close to check on her.

A WOMAN'S INTUITION

Chapter Sixteen

Present Day

Nautica drove down the highway heading toward her hotel. She glanced at the bag full of money next to her and smiled. She'd just met a man that she thought could be something, and in a new city, where she had no past demons to haunt her. *New city, new person.* She took a deep breath and got off on her exit.

She felt her phone vibrating and noticed that she had a couple of voice mails. She dialed her pin and began to check her messages. One message after the other one was from the girls at the strip club where she used to work, telling her that her boyfriend had been robbed. She had at least eight messages. They weren't telling her anything she didn't know about.

She began to go through more of her messages. She learned that Zion had died in the hospital from the gunshot wounds. She flipped down her phone and began to smile.

No more worries about Zion coming to find her. He'd killed Khia, and was right where he belonged. In a grave.

Just as Nautica was about to put her phone away, it vibrated. She looked at the caller ID. She took a deep breath and answered it, "Hello."

"Hey, Nautica," Benny said, as if he didn't pull that stunt the previous night.

"Hi," Nautica said with a heavy attitude.

"Look, I want to apologize for what happened last night. You know, I just got a little beside myself, and maybe you can forgive me somehow."

"Benny, I just want to forget about last night. We cool." She decided to play nice, remembering she wanted the part in the show.

"Cool. So I'll see you on the set Friday, right?" Benny said almost in a pleading tone.

"Of course, I'll be there."

"Okay, I guess I'll see you then. And another thing, Tical wasn't too mad after I left, was he?"

Nautica picked up on the fear in Benny's voice. "Everything's good. He didn't say too much about it." Nautica began to like Tical a little more. It was something about a feared man that turned her on. She was glad that Tical had intervened when he did, because she didn't know how it would've turned out.

"Cool," Benny said just before he hung up, relief in his voice.

Nautica had to study her lines for Friday, but first she had to think about what she would wear to the game later that night. Her mind drifted to the night she'd shared with Tical, and she felt warm inside at the very thought of him. She got out of the car and popped her trunk, grabbing her bag full of money. She wasn't going to let it out of her sight again. She went up to her hotel room to get ready for her date with Tical.

Nautica didn't know exactly what to wear to a football game, so she decided to go casual. Tight-fitting jeans that displayed her curves, a small black tank top, her hair neatly pulled back in a ponytail, and no makeup.

She felt special, never having been in a limo before. She sat in back of the limo that Tical had sent for her and looked at the lines of people piling up in front of the well-lit stadium to catch the Monday night game. The limo bypassed the massive line and headed through the VIP entrance.

"Here's your stop." The driver stepped out of the vehicle and walked around to let Nautica out.

Tical was standing at the entrance waiting for her, both hands in his pockets, looking handsome as ever. Crisp from head to toe, he wore a snug-fitting black sweater, loose-fitting black jeans, and a black knitted skullcap pulled down over his eyes. He didn't wear a chain, but his pinky ring was blinging. Nautica sashayed over and greeted him with a huge Kool-Aid smile.

Tical grinned and rubbed his hands together. "What up, ma?"

"Hello, Tical." She tip-toed and pecked him on the cheek.

Tical put his hands on Nautica's hips and looked her up and down. "You look beautiful." He nodded. He then grabbed her hand and guided her into the stadium's private entrance and through the long corridor that led to the elevator to his luxury box.

Nautica put on her lip gloss. *Damn, this nigga is fine.*

As they reached their floor, Tical glanced over at Nautica and winked at her, noticing how nervous she was.

Nautica smiled as the doors opened to the spacious box, where a waiter walked around with bottles and finger food. The box was equipped with plush carpet that matched the team colors, and the glass front that sat at the 50-yard line gave a perfect view of the field. People were scattered around talking and sipping on champagne.

It was a mixed crowd, half hood niggas, half business associates. Everyone stopped what they were doing to greet Tical when he entered with Nautica, who felt like a superstar on the red carpet. All eyes on them, it gave her a rush like no other.

Tical guided her through the crowd and over to the seats that sat right in front of the glass. He retrieved a bottle of champagne and two glasses from the waiter. He poured himself a glass. "You drinking with me?"

"Sure." She grabbed the other glass from Tical. "This is nice," she said, looking around.

"Yeah, I love coming here. I'm a big fan." Tical took a sip of his drink.

Nautica noticed that Tical was grilling her. She smiled. "What? I got lipstick on my teeth?" she said jokingly.

"Nah, it's just . . . never mind." Tical looked away.

"No. What? Tell me." Nautica nudged him.

"You're just so beautiful."

The sound of a woman's voice interrupted their moment.

"So are you going to introduce me to you new friend?" Millie walked around to their seats and stood in front of them.

"Oh, yeah. Millie, this is Nautica. Nautica, Millie." Tical waved an open hand toward Millie.

Millie extended her hand. "Nice to meet you."

Nautica shook her hand. "Same here. I've heard a lot about you." She examined the slim, chocolate-skinned girl and remembered her from the picture in Tical's home.

"Hope it was all good." Millie punched Tical in the arm. She stared at Nautica for a minute, but looked away before Nautica thought she was being rude. "Well, you guys, enjoy the game. I'ma go catch the game with Gunplay."

Nautica smiled and watched as Millie walked away. She felt like Millie was sizing her up, but brushed it off, not wanting to stir up anything. "So that's her, huh?"

"Yeah, that's my baby sis right there," he answered, his eyes focused on the field as the game kicked off.

Nautica automatically knew that they shared a bond from the way he talked about Millie, but it was something about the way Millie looked at Tical that gave off more than a sister/ brother relationship.

"So what's the scoop on her?" Millie said to Gunplay as she sipped on Grey Goose and cranberry on the rocks.

"She just a chick that he met the other night. She's an actress for the show or something." Gunplay glanced over at Tical and Nautica.

"Is that right?" Millie eyed Nautica down while taking a sip of her drink.

Tical was protective of Millie, but she was equally protective of him. She hated when sack chasers went after him. Tical usually didn't deal with gold diggers, but sometimes he let a few slip through the crack, and that's where she came in.

"She just probably another chick he's going to 'one-night.'" Millie smirked.

"Naw, shorty ain't like that. Seem like she got her shit together. She drive that new six series . . . like yours." Gunplay said in a instigating way, fucking with Millie. He knew how she felt about Tical and thought he'd have a little fun with her.

"Yeah, whatever, nigga." Millie smiled at Gunplay, knowing what he was doing. *I'ma keep my eye on her ass.* Millie felt a bad vibe from her. Tical was smiling and laughing, something he rarely did. She didn't want to admit it, but she was jealous. She knew that Nautica wasn't all she was cracked up to be. Call it a woman's intuition.

***

The game had just ended, and Nautica waited for Tical by the bar, sipping on a mixed drink. Tical stood by the door shaking each one of his business associate's hand as they walked out of the door. He embraced each of his henchmen on his squad as they walked out also as the room got more empty by the second. Gunplay and Millie were the last to leave.

Gunplay stopped counting the money he'd just won betting on the game with another hustler. "Yo, you want me to wait for you?"

"No, I'm good, fam. I will call you in the morning." Tical slapped hands with his best friend as he exited.

Millie followed close behind and hugged Tical as she left out the door. "See ya."

Tical closed the door behind her and focused his attention on Nautica. He walked over and sat next to her. He poured himself a glass of Hennessy on the rocks and patiently swirled the cup around, making the ice cubes clink. "Did you enjoy yourself?" He took a sip of his drink.

"Yeah, I really enjoyed myself, Tical." Nautica placed her hand on his chest. She was in awe of him. She witnessed him hold conversations with professionals such as doctors, lawyers, and bankers; but he also had conversations with grimy-looking goons and hustlers all night.

He gave her the right amount of attention that night to impress her. He wasn't all over her, but he kept her entertained and involved in conversation. He was a well-rounded man, and Nautica not only sat back and observed, but she learned. Tical was the type of man she dreamed about, and she wasn't going to let the opportunity slip through her hands.

Tical slid his hands into his pockets and gave her his boyish smile. "I was thinking . . . we should spend more time with each other. I'm a man that knows exactly what I want.

And I absolutely waste no time when going after something I desire."

Nautica blushed. She stuck her finger in her drink and stirred it. "Do you see something you want?" she asked, her eyes connecting with his.

Tical gently bit his bottom lip and nodded his head slowly. He walked even closer to her, till his chest was nearly touching her forehead.

The smell of his Unforgiven cologne tantalized Nautica's senses. She closed her eyes and rested her head on his midsection, his charm and magnetism overpowering her. She was tangled in his web. Nautica leaned in and let her lips touch his. The feeling of Tical's soft, warm lips sent a chill down her body that seemed to stop right at her clitoris, causing it to pulsate.

Tical put down his drink and placed his hand on the back of Nautica's neck. He slipped his tongue into her mouth. Nautica's body took over her mind, and before she knew it, her tight jeans were unbuttoned and she'd straddled him.

Tical, kissing her passionately, began to massage her breasts, making her nipples hard as nails. He stood up and removed his shirt, displaying his body, which was marked up like a subway station in Harlem. He didn't have a single space on his upper half that wasn't tattooed. Tical had over thirty-two tattoos, and that only turned Nautica on even more. She also took off her shirt and bra, displaying her perky, dark-circled breasts.

The two of them looked into each other's eyes while they undressed. Nautica had never experienced anything like it before. Of course, she'd had sex before, but this was intimacy.

Tical gently picked up Nautica and sat her on top of the bar, kissing her, moving his tongue in circles around hers. He dropped his jeans, exposing his curved rock-hard penis.

Nautica looked down, and her clitoris began to thump. She grabbed Tical's hot rod and began to stroke it. She had never experienced a man with a curve and was waiting in heavy anticipation.

Tical slid her jeans off and then her panties, while continuing to kiss her. She was so wet, a small puddle of her juices formed on the bar where she was sitting. She began to rub his tattooed body and spread her legs open, exposing her pinkness. When Tical plunged deep into her wound, a slurping noise filled the air, and they grunted in unison.

Nautica tensed up and dug her nails into Tical's ripped back. "Oooh," she whispered, flicking her tongue at his earlobe. Tical began to move his hips like a seasoned Latin dancer while inside Nautica, going at a steady pace. His curve hit the right spot every time, and his balls tickled Nautica's other hole every time he submerged. Nautica, in complete bliss, held on for dear life as he took her on the ride of her life with long, deep strokes.

"Boy, you gon' make me crazy," she whispered in his ear. She was already addicted to Tical's stroke.

Part Two:

Life of a Dopeman's Wife

UPGRADED

Chapter Seventeen

Nautica walked out onto the balcony of the plush hotel and watched the sun come up on Paris's beautiful skyline. The soft silk robe hugged her body, displaying all of her perfections, and she loved the way the soothing fabric felt against her skin. She took a deep breath, as the warmth of the rising sun graced her face. Tical and her had been in the France for the past six days, and she was having the best time of her life. *I am finally happy.* She ran her fingers through her hair. She wiped the sleep out of her eye and yawned, closing her eyes and enjoying the glamorous life.

As she stretched out her arms, she glanced at the huge rock on her finger that Tical had purchased for her just days before. He, without hesitation, dropped $5,200 on it when she mentioned that she fancied it. She wore it on her index finger and hoped that one day Tical would put one on her ring finger and make her his forever.

She had been inseparable with Tical for the past year. He had shown her how a woman was supposed to be treated.

Nautica was going into her second season at *The Wire*, and Tical had decided to take her on a trip before her hectic schedule began. She had done very well with the show and had gotten a bigger role because of her superb performance in the previous season. Everything was going right for her, and she was finally at peace. She left the hood and never looked back.

She had never mentioned her grimy past and planned on never telling him about her old lifestyle. She'd always thought, *What he doesn't know won't hurt him*, when thinking about her new image. Plus, Tical would always applaud her for being classy and would tell her he would never turn a ho into a housewife. He didn't approve of gold diggers and hot girls. Not wanting any connections to her old life whatsoever, she went as far as telling him that she was from Detroit, rather than Flint, which was only an hour away.

As Nautica was enjoying the incredible outlook, she was startled by a hand resting on her shoulder. She turned around and saw Tical's lean naked body before her.

"It's beautiful, isn't it?" he said, referring to the sunrise.

"Yeah, it is." Nautica ran her hand over Tical's washboard abdominal. Her hand drifted down to his manhood, and she began to fondle him. They'd made love most of the night, and Tical's curve had her wanting more. "I want some more of 'bo,'" she said, referring to the nickname she'd given his penis.

"Is that right?" Tical hugged her and began stroking her back.

"Yeah, that's right." Nautica kissed his chest, while holding bo in her hands. She stroked him until he became fully erect.

Tical turned Nautica around and ripped off her robe. He was aggressive, but just enough not to hurt her.

The morning air stiffened Nautica's nipples as Tical licked on the nape of her neck, sending tingles down her back. He slowly began to walk forward until Nautica reached the ledge.

She placed her hands on the rails, and Tical licked his fingertips and slid them down her ass crack and into her warm wound. She sucked her teeth in pleasure as Tical's two fingers entered her.

Tical stepped back and bent Nautica over. He grabbed bo and slid right into her from behind.

He took deep strokes, his wet thumb on her butt hole, and worked the middle as Nautica's behind bounced on his pelvis. Nautica sucked her own finger and moaned in almost a melodic tune as they became one.

After getting Nautica on the verge of an orgasm, Tical stopped and slid out of her. Bo's curve was at its fullest potential, and the sight stimulated Nautica even more. He walked over to the bed and lay flat on his back, and bo stood tall, like a leaning tower.

Nautica didn't waste any time hopping on top of him and guiding herself back on his pipe. She laid her chest flat on his and began to move her body in a slow wave.

Nautica's juices began to trickle down Tical's thighs as he gently palmed her buttocks, occasionally smacking it to let her know she was giving an A-1 performance.

Nautica thought about how much Tical had changed her life for the better. She didn't want or need for anything. She was making love to a powerful, loving man who would give her the world. "I love you, Tical," she whispered, tears flowing from her eyes onto Tical's cheek.

"I love you too. I love you so much, baby." Then he released himself inside his soul mate.

Nautica lay in Tical's arms as they rubbed each other, her body still tingling from the show Tical had just given her. "I don't want to leave Paris," she said, poking her lips.

"We'll come back in a couple of months." Tical wanted to stay too, but he had to return home to meet with Millie the next day, which was Friday.

"Yeah, right. We aren't going to have time. You are so busy, and I have the show and all."

"Lots of things are about to change. I am about to be done with the game, and I'll be focusing on different business ventures. And you."

"Are you serious?"

"Yeah, I'm dead serious. I just closed a deal for a club in downtown B-more. I think I'ma do that for a minute, you know. I'ma call it Eight One Four."

"Yeah, right!' Nautica sat up with a big smile. That was her birthdate.

"For real. Actually the grand opening is in two weeks. I'm hoping to focus on more business moves like that. The dope game isn't built for longevity. I've been eating in the streets for as long as I remember, and it's time for me to evolve. I'm going to pass the torch and go legit."

"What about Gunplay and Millie? What do they have to say about it? Are they giving it up too?"

Tical pinched Nautica's nose, impressed by her observation. He thought it was cute that she was being curious, but little did he know Nautica had dated, fucked, and played with hustlers all her life and wasn't green to the streets. "What you know about the streets?"

Nautica knew she'd said too much. "I'm just saying . . ."

"Not that you care, but I'm going to hand over the operation to them. I'm not going to stop their flow just because I decided to get out. I'ma let them eat by introducing them to my plug, and I'm going to put a strong team around them. They kept me on point and safe for all these years. Now I gotta make sure they have the same."

Nautica didn't say anything else. She was ready for him to get out of the game so they could start their life together without distraction.

CLUB 8-1-4
Chapter Eighteen

It was a hot Saturday night, and the air was just right for the official opening of Club 8-1-4. Tical invited all of his acquaintances from all regions of the country to come celebrate with him, and to offer them a position in Baltimore's drug trade. He was assembling a dominant squad for Millie and Gunplay to reign supreme.

Tical and Millie stood at the top of the balcony overlooking the mansion-style two-story club. The shiny marble floors and strobe lights gave the club a look of perfection, and the sounds of smooth R and B greeted the guests as they came in.

Tical thought about Nautica. She'd stayed home, not wanting to be in the spotlight. Which was one of the reasons he loved her so much. She wasn't a center-of-attention type person.

"This bitch getting packed already," Millie said, leaning on the rails, her back to the crowd. She'd decided to dress up for the occasion and wore a white dress that hugged her slim frame and displayed her small, plump behind. It was rare for her to even wear a dress.

"Yeah. It's a nice turnout." Tical raised his glass to the rapper on stage.

"Is that Jay?" Millie asked, referring to the international rap star from out of Brooklyn. His swagger kind of reminded her of Tical's.

Tical nodded his head modestly.

Millie smiled. Tical never ceased to amaze her. "How do you know him?"

Tical thought about the time he used to move bricks of cocaine and bundles of heroin back and forth from B-more to New York. "I used to handle business with him back in the day." He slipped one hand into his pocket and bobbed his head to the music.

"Handle business, huh?" Millie nodded knowingly.

That particular night was a special one. It was the anniversary date of the day that Tical changed Millie's life when he picked her up from the truck stop. Tical didn't keep up with the date, but Millie did.

Tical wore a three-piece suit to the event, but had his jacket off, only displaying his well-tailored shirt and vest. His necktie was loose, and he looked comfortable but debonair. He always looked at her like a younger sister, but Millie wanted him to look at her the same way he did

Nautica. Millie couldn't help but to stare at the man before her.

Tical took a sip of his drink and matched Millie's stare. He placed his hand on her face and smirked.

Millie closed her eyes and moved her cheek against his warm palm as it rested gently on her. "Tical, I love you," she said, opening her eyes. When Tical leaned in to kiss her, her heart fluttered. The day she'd been waiting on for years had finally arrived. She closed her eyes and puckered her lips.

"I love you too, baby sis." Tical pecked her on the forehead and patted her back.

Millie was disappointed and embarrassed. She thought her dreams were coming true.

Tical saw Gunplay on the dance floor, a female grinding on him. He waved for him to come up the stairs. "Yo, Millie, I have to talk to you and Gunplay in my office. I'll be waiting in there." He smiled and pinched her cheek. "You're growing up," he said, looking her up and down. He thought she looked so sexy.

Millie crossed her arms and gave him a fake smile. As Tical disappeared into his office, she took a deep breath, waiting for Gunplay to come join her.

Nautica walked around her home she shared with Tical in a comfortable BCBG sweat suit, her hair pulled back and wrapped with a rubber band. She loved the way the plush carpet felt between her toes. She had convinced Tical to turn Millie's room into a study, since she wasn't using the room, so she'd have a comfortable place in the house to read and act out her lines for the show. She was preparing to move Millie's stuff to the garage.

Actually, Nautica was happy to get Millie's things out of *her* house. *I don't really care for her ass anyway.* She took Millie's pictures off the wall and placed them inside a big cardboard box. Millie wasn't rude to Nautica over the past year, but it was obvious she didn't like that Tical and her were in a serious relationship. I don't know what her problem is. I ain't did shit to the bitch. She walk around her with her nose all turned up and shit. I know when a bitch trying to act funny. Shit, I ain't the one."

After two hours of hard work, Nautica fanned herself from all the moving and organizing. She'd made at least eight trips to the garage. She wanted to keep busy while Tical was hosting his grand opening party at his new club. She wanted to go so bad, but with the picture she'd painted of herself for Tical, there was no turning back. Tical always told her how much he couldn't stand sheisty females, and would always praise her for her nobility and her sophistication. He really believed she didn't like to party, was green to the streets, and had only had sex with two other men her whole entire life. All big lies. *Will he look at me differently if I tell him about my past? Will he still love a liar and a thief?* She sat on the bed.

In the beginning Nautica had her own money and didn't need a nigga for anything, but little did Tical know, she was working with another hustler's blood money. Nautica nearly ran through all of the money she'd stolen from Zion within the first three months, to keep up with Tical's lifestyle, but eventually they got close and all of her worries were over. The money she made from the show was chump change, compared to the stacks Tical gave her. Tical made her wifey and took care of her. He used to joke with her and say, "Just sit back and look pretty." And actually that was all she had to do.

Tical sat in his oversized executive chair and swirled back and forth in his luxury office with a glass front overlooking the club. He also had security monitors built into his desk, so he could see what was going on in and out of the club. He walked over to the marble table in the rear of his office and pushed a button that prompted a mini-bar to rise from the marble counter.

One of the out-of-town soldiers looked on in amazement. "That's like some James Bond shit."

Tical smirked as he poured himself a glass of cognac over ice. He unbuttoned his diamond cufflinks and slightly rolled up his sleeves before grabbing the glass and taking a sip. He looked at the two men that sat in front of his desk, both from different regions of the country, and both deadly killers. He'd called on them to assist Millie and Gunplay with the "new era" in Baltimore. He leaned against the counter, waiting for Millie and Gunplay to join the meeting.

Though the club area was distant, Tical could feel the bass pumping. "I gotta get this office soundproofed," he said, bobbing his head to Jay's new song that was blasting.

"Tical, it's been a long time. I think the last time I saw you was at Zion's funeral," the man said.

"Yeah, Loon, it's been a while." Tical walked to his desk and leaned on the edge of it, right in front of them. "How you been?"

"I'm good. Flint dry as hell right now, though. Ain't shit moving that way." Loon rubbed his hands together, still excited about the phone call he'd received from Tical a couple weeks back.

"Well, that's news of old. I brought you here to get money. I owe that much to my man Zion."

"Yeah, Zion thought highly of you," Loon said, rubbing the scraggly beard he'd grown.

"Yeah, I tend to think about him from time to time. We did good business together."

Tical used to supply Zion. He remembered Zion talking about Loon's loyalty and instantly thought about him when he began assembling his new team.

Church, the other guy in the room, was the son of Black Pete, a Haitian drug boss out of Miami who Tical did a two-year stretch with in Attica. Tical noticed how closely he resembled his father. Black Pete was connected to the Black Zulu Gang, a ruthless cartel that originated from Haiti. Fifteen years Tical's senior, Black taught him a lot about the drug game throughout his bid. Black Pete and Tical kept in touch, and Black Pete told Tical his young son was getting wild in Miami and that the police was on him for all the bodies he'd caught over the past two summers. Tical told him he would let him know if ever he had room for Church to come and join his squad in B-more.

As Millie and Gunplay walked in, Tical went to sit behind his desk. "Have a seat," he told them.

Millie looked at the two guys in the room and wondered what was going on. "Who is these niggas?" She pointed at both of them.

Church said, "Who the fuck you talking to?"

"Nigga, you better hold ya mu'fuckin' horses." Gunplay ice-grilled both guys.

"Play nice." Tical chuckled. "I see you guys all get along. Millie, Gunplay, I want you to meet Loon and Church." Tical waved his hand toward the two. "Church is from Miami, and I am real tight with his old man. Gunplay, you remember Black Pete? This is his son."

"Oh, yeah! Pete's good people."

"And this is Loon. He is a shooter, understand? This was my man's Zion little man. I want y'all to embrace them, because they'll be sticking around for a minute."

Gunplay turned up his nose at Loon. Zion was a stickup kid. And Gunplay never cared too much for him, because he hated thieves. But Gunplay knew Zion and Tical used to be tight, so out of respect, he was going to be cordial. "What up, fam?"

Loon threw up his head in greeting.

Millie stared at the two guys. "Tical, what do we need these niggas for? I mean, we got the streets on lock right now. Plus, I don't even know these mu'fuckas."

"Calm down, Millie. It's time for you to get out the streets and start running this operation. If you're trying to be boss, you can't do what you used to do. You can't get your hands dirty and be in the trap like you used to be. It's time to step up your game and become untouchable. These two soldiers are going to allow you to do that. They're going to be your face, sort of like spokespersons. You get it?"

Millie stared at Loon and was totally disgusted by his appearance. His pasty, light skin, reddish hair, and freckles gave him a deranged look, and Church, five foot six and black as tar, wasn't that impressive either. But, she knew Tical was trying to make sure the transition was smooth, so she was going to embrace them.

SMALL WORLD

Chapter Nineteen

Nautica sat back and looked over the room that she'd just completely remodeled within hours. Wet and sweaty from all the moving, she decided to get in the shower, to be fresh when her man came home. She was looking forward to seeing bo that night. She glanced at the clock. It was just a few minutes after 2:00 A.M. *Tical should be here any minute.*

Nautica slipped out of her clothes and went to the bathroom. The walk-in shower was made of glass, so she was able to watch the local news on the TV that hung from the wall in the corner of the spacious bathroom as she showered.

Tical and his entourage walked into his house talking about the night's happenings. He'd invited his crew, old and new, back to his place after the party. Millie, Gunplay, Church, and Loon went into the den.

"This is a nice crib," Church said as he looked around and sat down on the big comfortable sectional.

Tical grabbed a bottle of Belvedere from his bar and five shot glasses from his cabinet. He walked over to join everyone else and began to pour the cups full and everyone grabbed a glass. He raised his glass. "This is to a new era and a flawless operation."

Everyone else raised their glass as well and took the shot.

Just as Tical wiped his mouth, he heard Nautica's heels clicking down the porcelain stairs.

Nautica heard noise downstairs, so she knew Tical had made it in. She smiled as she sat in her vanity mirror and stroked her hair with a brush. She wore a silk nightgown and slipped on her six-inch stilettos that Tical loved so much. She always walked around the house with the heels, knowing it turned her man on.

She stood up, with her robe open, and looked at her nude body. She began to rub baby oil on her body everywhere, except on her vagina. She didn't want Tical to taste anything but her natural juices. She closed her robe and headed downstairs to greet her man, making her steps loud so that the sound of her heels clicking echoed throughout the house.

As she made it to the last step, Tical was standing in the entrance of the den, smiling at her. "Hey, beautiful," he said, leaning against the doorway, hands in his pockets. His sleeves were rolled up a bit, showing his tatted forearms.

"Hey, baby." Nautica lit up. She loved the way he looked in his loose tie and unbuttoned dress shirt. And the way his shoulders filled out his shirt. Not to mention the slight bulge in his dress pants, which only made her love button begin to thump.

Nautica opened her robe, exposing her neatly trimmed bush and oiled body. Tical eyes got big as he rushed over to her. He quickly closed her robe. "We have company, girl."

"Sorry, baby." She hugged Tical, as they both shared a laugh. She glanced toward the den but couldn't see because of the dipping stairs that led to it.

Tical kissed her passionately. "Go slip on some clothes, so I can introduce you."

"Okay, just give me a minute."

As Nautica made her way back up the stairs, Tical kept his eyes glued to her backside, her fat ass shifting from side to side. He shook his head and returned to the den.

Minutes later Nautica returned downstairs and headed into the den. She could hear the music playing from the surround sound speakers. She entered the den and saw Tical, Gunplay, Millie and—"Oh my God," she whispered. Her breaths became shallow, and her heart skipped a beat. She saw Loon looking directly at her. The pale skin and freckly face was like a shot to the head for her.

"There you go, babygirl. Come in and let me introduce you to my peoples."

Nautica walked toward Tical, a confused expression all over her face. *What the fuck is going on? Oh my God.*

Tical placed his hand on the small of her back. "Nautica, this is Loon and Church. They are going to be around here for a while."

Loon clenched his jaws as he stared at Nautica. He'd been looking for her for over a year. He thought he was dreaming, but he looked closer and confirmed that it was her. He stood up, his eyes still on her. He quickly turned his frown into a smile and extended his hand. "Hello. It's nice to meet you. You look very familiar," Loon said as he walked in front of her. The last time he'd seen her was in the hotel room with Khia and Zion. Loon squeezed her hand tight, but Nautica didn't flinch.

"You probably saw her on TV. She's a actress for *The Wire*. My baby talented." Tical smiled and winked his eye at Nautica.

Nautica, her hands soaking wet out of fear and nervousness, remained silent as she shook his hand.

"Oh yeah, baby," Tical said, "he's from Flint. That's like only an hour away from where you are from, right?"

"Yeah, something like that." Nautica pulled her hand away from Loon and put on a forced smile.

"It's a small world, huh." Loon looked at Nautica without even blinking, his blood boiling.

"Yeah, small world," Nautica said almost in a whisper.

Tical looked over at Church. "And this is my man Church. Me and his family go way back."

"What's good, ma? Nice to meet you." Church put two fingers up and continued to sip on his drink.

Gunplay looked up from rolling a spliff. "What up, sis?"

"Hey, Gunplay." Nautica was terrified at that point, not knowing what the hell Loon was doing there and how he knew Tical. "Hey, Millie," she said, trying to not let her uneasiness show.

Millie threw her head up, not really wanting to acknowledge Nautica.

"Nautica spoke to you," Tical said with a slightly raised voice, like a father telling his daughter to straighten up.

Millie put on a phony smile. "Hello. How are you, Nautica?"

Nautica turned to Tical and laid her hands on her chest. "Baby, I just came down to speak. I'm about to go upstairs and go to sleep."

"Okay, baby, I will be up after everyone leaves." Tical kissed her on her forehead.

When Nautica turned to leave, she heard Loon say, "It was nice meeting you."

She shot up the stairs in complete bewilderment.

Nautica, her mind racing and her hands shaking, paced the bedroom back and forth, not knowing what to do or think. She whispered, "Oh my God! Oh my God! Oh my God!"

"I gotta use the bathroom." Gunplay took another shot.

The whole crew had been drinking and playing dominoes for about an hour, and everyone was wasted. Except for Loon. His mind was focused on how in the hell he stumbled upon Nautica. He barely watched TV, so he'd never noticed her on the show, or ever thought to look outside of Flint.

At first, murderous thoughts went through his head, but when he saw how much Tical cared about Nautica, he began to get other thoughts. He was going to make her suffer before killing her.

"Yo, I gotta use the john too. You got a spare bathroom?" Loon stood up.

Tical stopped shuffling the dominoes and pointed toward the stairs. "Yeah, upstairs. First door to your right."

"Cool."

Loon went up to the second level and saw the bedroom light on. He slowly crept toward the bedroom and peeked in. Nautica was taking off her clothes and slipping into some nightwear. He always wanted to sex her. He walked in without her noticing, grabbed her from behind, and kissed her neck.

Nautica smiled. "What took you so long?" She backed her ass into him. She quickly jumped back when she realized it wasn't Tical holding her.

"What? Not who you expected?"

Nautica looked into the hall to make sure no one else was there. "What the fuck are you doing here?" she asked in a harsh whisper.

"I'm the one who's asking all the questions, bitch! I was there the night you and that bitch killed Zion. I also got that shit on tape." Loon looked at her intensely.

"Liar," she said, not believing him.

"Am I lying? How would I know that you and Khia killed him, huh? I was in the closet taping the whole thing."

"Oh my God!" Nautica put her hand over her mouth, and her eyes got watery.

"Don't worry. I'm not going to tell Tical. Zion did a lot of dirt. His past was bound to catch up with him anyway."

Nautica continued to check the door. "So what the fuck do you want from me?"

"I'm staying in the Inner Harbor's Holiday Inn, Room 731. Meet me there five o'clock sharp tomorrow, and we'll talk then. If your ass don't show up, I'ma let Tical know about his sweet li'l wifey. And maybe I'll send a copy of the tape to the police. Yeah, I think I might do that." Loon felt good having Nautica wrapped around his finger. "Meet me there or else," he said just before returning downstairs to join the crew.

CREEPING WITH THE ENEMY
Chapter Twenty

Chills went down Nautica's back as she stood in front of Room 731 and prepared to knock on Loon's hotel door. Everything inside of her was telling her to leave, but the thought of Tical finding out about her past plagued her. She hesitantly knocked on the door and waited for a response. Moments later the door opened, and Loon stood there with baggy jeans and a wife-beater. He looked Nautica up and down like she was a piece of meat, as he played with the toothpick hanging out from his mouth. He stepped to the side so she could walk in.

Nautica entered the room, wondering what was next.

Loon always wanted a dime piece, but his appearance never allowed him to do so. In fact, he'd never had sex with a woman without paying for it and was hot and ready. And as Nautica stood in front of him, he only had one thing on his mind. He had something over her head and was going to make the most of it before killing her. He stared at her hips. "I'm glad you could make it."

Nautica gave him a look of total repulsion, her arms crossed tight. "What the fuck did you tell me to come here for, Loon?"

"I just want to taste you." Loon licked his lips and dropped to his knees.

Nautica looked at him like he was crazy. "Fuck that!"

"You sure about that?" he asked sarcastically, his eyes on her pussy print, only thinking about having oral sex with her.

"You a sick mu'fucka!" Nautica turned and headed for the door.

"Nautica! I want you to see something." Loon walked over to the television and clicked it on.

Nautica's eyes shot to the screen, where she and Khia were wrapped up in a sixty-nine position. Tears began to form in her eyes. She unbuttoned her pants, pulled it down, and let Loon have his way with her.

THREE MONTHS AFTER THE STORM

Chapter Twenty-one

Nautica lay on her belly and let the sun beam on her back as she rested comfortably on Tical's gigantic yacht, shades covering her eyes, her two-piece Burberry swimsuit hugging her curves. The shot looked like a scene out of a rap video.

Reading over her script for the following week's shoot, she was having a hard time concentrating. She couldn't block Loon out of her head. It had been three months since he'd been blackmailing her, and he'd had oral sex with her five times, including the first time in his hotel room. *I wish somebody would kill that nigga. I can't just keep on letting him do whatever to me. It got to be another way for me to make this shit go away.* She put her script down and sipped on her piña colada.

It was New Year's Eve, and Tical had invited everyone on the yacht that particular Sunday. He had a big celebration planned at the club later that night, but they started the party early amongst themselves on the yacht. Uncomfortable with Loon's presence on the yacht, Nautica chose to stay on the top deck away from everyone else. Whenever she was in the same room with Loon and Tical, she got jittery, thinking Loon would bust her out at any moment. She desperately hoped that Tical and her could hurry and leave Baltimore like they'd been planning.

Nautica had to use the restroom, so she headed to the bottom deck, where the bathroom was. As she was heading back up to the top deck, Loon was coming down the stairs with a bottle of champagne, and eyes red from the purple haze he'd been smoking. He backed her down the stairs.

Nautica tensed up and tried to avoid looking in his eyes. "Loon, not here."

Loon grew horny at the thought of Tical being so close while he was about to have his way with his woman. "You do what I say when I say." He gripped her arm and began to kiss her neck sloppily.

"Stop, Loon," she said in a harsh whisper. She tried to push him away, but he was too strong for her.

"You know you want it." Loon bit her earlobe and pulled her closer to him by her waist.

Nautica struggled with him and laid a hard slap on his face, causing him to release her. She almost regretted it.

Loon grabbed his face. He grinned. "I like it rough. I'll see you later on," he said as he headed back up the stairs to the deck area.

Nautica balled up her fist. "I can't do this shit," she said, clenching her jaws.

She walked up to the deck and straightened up her bikini top, which Loon had slightly twisted. When she looked up, Gunplay was standing right there. She quickly headed to the third deck, hoping he didn't see Loon down there with her.

Chapter Twenty-two

Loon leaned his head into the notebook and used his nose as a vacuum to sniff the line of blow. He quickly jerked his head back to prevent his nose from running as he passed the notebook over to Church, who rolled up a bill and snorted the other line, which Loon had prepared for him.

Loon thumbed his nose as he looked at the people going into Tical's club. "Okay, tonight's the night." He looked over at Church, whose eyes watered because of the potency of the drug.

"I'm ready. It's our time to be top dog," Church said, repeating what Loon had been telling him all week.

Loon had finally persuaded Church to kill Tical, telling him that as long as Tical was alive, they would never be able to come into their own. Loon also wanted Nautica, but knew he would never get her heart while Tical was still breathing. At first he was just using Nautica for his sexual satisfaction, but along the way he fell in love with her. In his mind, Nautica loved him too. He knew by the way she twitched when he ate her out that she was enjoying it.

She'll come around. I just have to get Tical out of the way so that she can get her focus off that nigga. I am going to knock him off, then Millie and Gunplay. This city is going to be mine. I'm the mu' fuckin' man! Not Tical. Loon's mind was getting more twisted and deranged by the day, and the only thing he knew for sure was that he was in love with Nautica and was determined to make her his forever.

"So, look, I'm going to keep everyone downstairs, and I want you to hit him at twelve midnight, while everyone is in the club doing the countdown. I don't want any mistakes. Load that nigga up with the whole clip. I want him dead by twelve 'o one, ya dig? Drop the gun and return to the party like nothing happened."

"I got you, Loon. I'ma wet that nigga up something serious." Church emptied the small baggie's contents onto the notebook to vacuum another pile. "What about Millie and Gunplay?"

"I'ma take care of them. You just take care of Tical, and everything else will fall in place." Loon had planned to kill Church later that night. "You ready to come up, my nigga?" He held out his fist for a pound from Church.

"I'm ready." Church pulled out his 9 mm and screwed on the silencer.

Tical looked out onto the packed club as he sipped on a small glass of cognac. Nautica stood behind him rubbing his chiseled chest. She remained silent as Tical was in deep thought and mute. She had flashes of what happened the previous night with Loon. *I hate him. I let him degrade me.* She thought about telling Tical the truth, so Loon's game could finally end. But the more she thought about coming clean, the more she thought about losing Tical.

Nautica continued to rub his chest. "Baby, it's New Year's Eve. You need to relax. You don't seem like yourself tonight," she said, finally breaking the silence.

"For some strange reason, I have a funny feeling about tonight. I don't know why, but I do." Tical stared out the glass. True hustlers always had a sixth sense, and Tical's was kicking in. Something just wasn't right, and he was trying to put his finger on it.

"Everything is going to be okay. You're probably just stressed out, ya know."

"Yeah, you're probably right." Tical turned around and slid his hands onto her hips. He leaned down and kissed her, and she wrapped her arms around his neck.

When they finished kissing, Tical walked behind his desk and began to look at the cameras. He just wanted to keep a cautious eye on what was happening inside his club.

Nautica looked at the clock and noticed it was 11:30. "Baby, it's almost time for the countdown."

Loon walked through the club wearing all black and a do-rag tied tight around his head. He headed toward the back entrance to let Church inside. He didn't want anyone to see Church until after the hit. He made his way past Millie and Gunplay, who sat in the VIP section popping bottles and partying. They were so busy having fun, they didn't see Loon slip past. Loon went to the back near the restroom and opened the door, letting Church in. Church also had on all black and a hat pulled down tight over his eyes.

Loon entered the club area and saw Nautica coming down the stairs. He went over to her, so he could meet her at the last step. He grabbed her hand. "What's up, baby?"

"Bitch, don't baby me!" Nautica pulled her hand back and looked to see if anyone was watching.

"I see you're feisty. You'll come around in due time."

Nautica rolled her eyes and brushed past him as she headed toward the VIP section, where she was supposed to wait for Tical. She went over to Gunplay and grabbed a bottle of champagne from the table.

Gunplay saw the frustration in her face. "You good?"

"Yeah, I'm good."

Loon walked up and slapped hands with Millie and Gunplay before he sat in the booth.

Gunplay took another swig of his drink. "Where is Tical?"

Nautica leaned into Gunplay, trying to be heard over the music. "He's upstairs in the office. He is on his way down, he looking over some papers."

Gunplay nodded his head and began rocking to the club banger.

Church tried to be as inconspicuous as possible as he went up the stairs and headed to Tical's office. He gripped the gun inside the front pocket of his hoody as he approached the door.

Tical was sitting at his desk going over the papers for the release of the rights to the show, when he saw Church slide in. "Nigga, knock before you come in my shit. Fuck is yo' problem?" Tical, his face frowned, shook his head and glanced back down at his papers. "What you want anyway?"

Church remained silent as he walked closer to Tical.

"Nigga, may I help you?"

Church pulled out the gun.

"What you going to do with that?" Tical said calm and collectively.

Church held up the gun and pointed it at Tical. His hands shaking as he aimed the weapon, he finally looked into Tical's eyes. Although Church was the one with the gun, he was the more fearful. A brief silence filled the room as the two men stared at each other, neither moving a muscle.

Church finally let off five slugs into Tical's chest, and Tical flew backwards in his chair and lay their motionless, his eyes closed. Tical was gone. Church ran out of the office and straight into the bathroom, not believing what he'd just done. He splashed water onto his face and smiled. It was his time to come up in the game.

TICAL'S DEATH

Chapter Twenty-three

Nautica looked around for Tical as the crowd counted down the new year. *Where's my baby at?* She saw Loon staring at her as if she was the only person in the room. She then saw Church scooting into the booth, and Loon handed him a bottle. Church whispered into Loon's ear, causing him to smile.

"Five, four, three, two, one—happy new year!" the crowd erupted, as balloons dropped from the ceiling and fell onto the huge dance floor.

Nautica continued to search the crowd for her man, but she didn't see him. She looked up to his office, expecting him to be observing the dance floor as he always did, but she still didn't see him. When she got up to go see what the holdup was, she felt a hand grab her and pull her back down.

"Where you going? Not to that nigga, I hope."

"Why are you grabbing me like that in front of all these people, Loon?" Nautica pulled back from him.

Millie and Gunplay were too busy popping bottles to notice him grab her up. Nautica quickly scanned the room for Tical. She saw him coming through the crowd with just a wifebeater on. She quickly scooted over, trying to create space between her and Loon before her man saw it.

Luckily Tical was wearing a bulletproof vest and the bullets didn't go through. He maneuvered through the crowd, a pistol gripped in his right hand, causing people to created a path for him. He was headed directly toward the booth. Neither Loon or Church saw him approaching. He grabbed Church by the neck and put a big chrome .45-pistol in his mouth. "You can't kill me, li'l nigga!"

Instantly Millie and Gunplay stood up to see what was going on.

"Baby, what's going on?" Nautica asked.

Tical then pulled the gun out of Church's mouth and fired three shots into the air, causing the whole club to scamper. He wanted to clear out the club, so there wouldn't be any witnesses. The club went into pandemonium as everyone scrambled for the exit.

Millie and Gunplay pulled out their guns, trying to find out what was happening.

Within a minute, the entire club was empty, and the sound of tires screeching erupted from the parking lot.

Gunplay stood next to Tical, who had a scared Church by his neck, choking the life out of him. "What's wrong, fam?"

"This nigga just tried to murk me!"

Gunplay put his gun to Church's head, and so did Millie.

Church yelled, "It wasn't my idea!"

Loon was shook to death, not believing Tical was alive. He had to act quick before Church told it all. Without hesitation, he pulled out his pistol and sent two bullets through Church's head, forcing his brains through the other side that he shot from. Everyone looked in shock as Church lay slumped. Tical released his corpse and let off two more in his body.

"Nobody goes against the team!" Loon said, breathing heavily. He looked at Tical, trying to read him.

"Loon, call the cleaners!" Tical took off his bloody wife-beater. "And take Nautica home when you done." He stormed off toward his office, followed closely by Gunplay and Millie.

Loon hit the steering wheel as he thought about his failed attempt on Tical's life. "Fuck!"

Nautica hesitantly got in the car and scooted as far away as she could from him. Scared for Tical, she didn't know what to think. She'd tried to talk to him, but he told her to just go home, he'd meet her there later.

As they pulled into Tical's driveway, Nautica quickly opened the door to get out, but Loon grabbed her by the arm and pulled her back down into the seat. Then he quickly unleashed his grip when he saw the look on her face. He knew his time was running thin with her, and eventually she would get tired of him blackmailing her.

His bipolar mind was playing tricks on him. He really thought he could get Nautica to love him like she loved Tical. He looked into her eyes and caressed her face. "Look, let's just run away together. I will treat you like the beautiful queen you are."

Nautica jerked back and frowned. "Look, Loon, you will never be Tical, okay. Never! I would never want to be with you. Even if you were the last nigga on earth." She got out of the car and headed toward the house.

Heartbroken, Loon pulled off devising a plan in his mind.

The next day Tical was in deep contemplation at his desk, wondering what would make Church turn on him. He'd had a sleepless night. *Who the fuck am I keeping in my circle?* He been reevaluating his decision making. Nautica was acting strange lately, Millie had an ongoing attitude with him, and he kept battling back and forth about leaving the game alone.

Tical was supposed to have made his exit from the streets months ago, but he always thought, *one more month. One more flip.* See, drug dealing was addictive too, and the lure of fast money was as powerful as the urge to shoot heroin or smoke crack.

He answered his phone, "Yo." Weed smoke still in his lungs, he made smoke circles as he leaned back in his chair and waited for a response.

"Loyalty is what separate boys from men, Tical. I taught you that many, many years ago," a voice with a thick Haitian accent said.

Tical immediately recognized the voice as Black Pete's, his former mentor. He'd been expecting the call all morning. "He went against the grain."

"He was my flesh and blood and now I must bury him into the ground while you remain on this earth, Tical."

Tical wanted to be apologetic, but that would be no good to Black Pete. He'd already crossed the line. "Let's quit the bullshit, Black. You know where I'm at. I love you with all my heart, but I will put you right next to yo' kid, if that's what you want." He took another deep pull of the spliff.

"I'm sorry to hear that you feel that way, Tical. I loved you like a son, but not more than MY son," Black said, his voice becoming more aggressive with each word. "I will see you soon, my friend." He hung up.

Tical blew out the smoke and sat back in his chair. He knew that was a threat.

Just then Nautica walked in with her big Chanel purse and long black pea coat, and it seemed that all his troubles went out the window. He unleashed that smile of his, snuffing out the spliff in the ashtray.

"Hey," Nautica said. She'd just left the set of the show and was glad to be home. Witnessing Church's murder the previous night had been on her mind all day.

"Hey, beautiful. How was your day?"

"I should be asking you that." She pulled her shades to the top of her head and walked behind Tical and massaged his shoulders.

Tical, his eyes closed, moved his neck in a circular motion. "That feels good, baby. You always make shit better, you know that?"

"That's what I'm here for. You seem like you have a lot on your mind." She kissed the top of his head.

Tical grabbed Nautica and sat her on his lap. "I'm glad I have you. Throughout all of this, I know everything is going to be all right as long as I got you and you got me. I know regardless of what everybody else do, you got my back. I'm surrounded by liars and envious mu'fuckas. I just need you to promise me one thing." He pulled away from her, so he could look into her eyes.

"Anything."

"Never lie to me or be untrustworthy. It seems like you are the only thing that is for sure in my life."

Nautica couldn't help thinking about the things she'd been lying to him about, not to mention allowing Loon to be intimate with her behind his back. She stared into his eyes and cradled his face. "I won't." She kissed his lips softly.

Just then Tical heard his alarm beep, signaling that the front door had been opened. He eased Nautica off his lap and looked at her and put his finger over his lips, telling her to remain quiet. Nautica had no idea what was going on.

He reached into his desk and grabbed his gun and crept toward the living room. He clicked his gun off safety. He saw a shadow and swung his gun at the intruder.

"Ahhhh!" Millie put both of her hands up. "Damn, Tical! What the fuck you got guns on me and shit for?"

"Damn, Millie, you should of knocked, coming into my shit!"

"Why would I knock and I have a key?" Millie closed the door and shook her head.

Tical lowered his gun and put it in the small of his back as he returned to the den with Nautica. "It's cool, baby. It was just Millie."

Millie followed close behind. *Just Millie?*

"Oh, you scared me." Nautica sat down.

"Damn, Tical! I been coming in with a key for years." Millie sat across from Nautica.

Tical walked to the bar and poured him some cognac over ice. "Yeah, well, you need to start letting a nigga know you coming over. Got that?" Tical was expecting to see one of Black Pete's Haitians creeping in to try to kill him.

Millie began to sulk. Tical had never used that tone with her. She knew Nautica was the reason for the sudden change. "Okay, whatever. I just came to drop off this money from the last shipment and get my holster from my room." She stormed upstairs.

Tical began to feel bad, knowing Millie was only catching a backlash from everything going on with him. He didn't mean to raise his voice at her. "Damn!" he whispered. He drank down the whole glass and slammed it on the bar. He walked over to his desk and put his gun back in his desk.

"She seems hot." Nautica smiled on the inside. Millie would finally see her room rearranged.

On cue, Millie stormed down the stairs and stood in the doorway, hands on her hips. "Tical, where is all my stuff?" she asked almost in tears. She never really had nothing to call her own before Tical gave her that room, and seeing Nautica's belongings in there really tore her up.

"In the garage."

"In the garage?" Millie looked at Tical like he was crazy.

Tical remained silent. He forgot that he'd told Nautica she could turn Millie's room into a study.

"You acting like a mu'fuckin' cake-ass nigga right now!"

Tical sat down in his chair, his face frowned up. He'd never expected her to come at him like that. "It's time for you to grow up, baby."

"No. It's time for *you* to grow up. You all up this bitch ass. What happened to you, Tical?" Millie fought back tears.

Nautica jumped up and snapped her neck back, going ghetto on Millie's ass. "Who the fuck is you calling a bitch!"

"Bitch, don't make me put a slug through that ass."

Tical instantly went between the two girls as they charged each other. He grabbed Nautica and whispered in her ear.

Nautica quickly calmed down. "Well, you need to get that li'l girl."

"I got your little girl right here." Millie ran up on Nautica, reaching over Tical.

Tical grabbed her by the shoulders and shook her. "Look, you outta line, Millian!"

"You going to put this bitch over me, Tical? Huh? Well, fuck you, nigga! You letting pussy control your actions. You know what!" Millie pulled away from him. "Fuck you! Fuck both of y'all. Y'all deserve each other." And she left out, holding up her middle finger.

Tical had never experienced such disrespect. If it was anybody else, he would have put a bullet through their body. He went upstairs, leaving Nautica alone in the den. He shook his head when he heard his front door slam. *She's getting out of hand.*

Nautica mumbled to herself, "That bitch is going to be a problem."

SEX, LIES, AND A TAPE

Chapter Twenty-four

Loon took another shot of the Patrón as Millie ran the bills through the money machine. He licked his lips, wondering how she looked with no clothes on. He knew, under that tough exterior, she had a sensual side, and was dying to see it. That's why he suggested they count the money at his spot rather than the dope spot they usually counted at.

Millie was so busy putting rubber bands on the money as they came out of the machine, she didn't notice Loon staring at her. "Pour me a shot, nigga."

Millie finally noticed the look in Loon's eyes. She quickly smacked her lips, dismissing any thought he might've had at that moment. She promised that the next man she dealt with would reflect Tical, nothing less. She pulled the small-caliber pistol from her waist and sat it on the table. She took the shot Loon had poured for her.

"Millie, can I ask you a question?" Loon poured both of them another shot.

She nodded.

"Why you so loyal to Tical? I mean, you got the whole east side locked, and if you get your own connect, you could take over. I never met a bitch like you. You got a chance to be head dopeman—dope-woman." Loon downed his shot.

"What the fuck you mean?" Millie stopped rubber-banding the stack of money. "You got some nerve, nigga. How can you fix yo' mouth to say some bullshit like that? That's what wrong with niggas—too many chiefs, not enough Indians."

Loon regretted exposing his cards to Millie. Tired of being a worker and ready to come up by any means necessary, his goal was to take out Tical after he gained more clout throughout the city. He just wanted to test the waters, to see if Millie would be a part of his takeover. He giggled, trying to play it off. "I'm just bullshitting."

Nautica was breathing heavily as she lay on the satin sheets, her body glowing with sweat. She was smiling because of the sexual performance Tical had just laid down, and her love button was still sensitive to the touch. She was admiring Tical's chiseled back and tight buttocks as he walked over to his safe behind the Bob

Marley portrait and began to pull out stacks of money and toss them into the bag that sat at his feet.

Nautica, being the natural hustler, had already peeped game. Tical, not wanting to have too much money in one spot at once, would always empty his safe before Millie came and dropped off the week's profit. Tical never would expect Nautica to be so street savvy. Nautica even knew his combination by heart, because she always paid attention when he opened it.

"Baby, I'm going to the West Coast for a couple of days to do some business. Are you going to be all right here by yourself?"

Nautica's phone lit up on the nightstand. The volume was turned off, so Tical didn't realize she was getting a call.

She picked it up. *Fuck!* She quickly sent Loon to voice mail and slipped the phone under her pillow.

"I hate when you leave me. How long are you going to be gone?"

"Just a couple of days. You going to miss me?" He closed the safe and put the portrait back up.

"Of course, I am."

Tical stared at Nautica's beautiful temple and knew he could spend the rest of his life with her. She was everything he wanted in a woman. That was the exact reason why he was about to fly to Beverly Hills to pick up a rare diamond that a famous jeweler had made especially for her. He had told a small lie about going to the West Coast for business, just so she wouldn't get suspicious. He was ready to pop the question and make her his official girl.

Tical glanced at the clock. It was almost five, and it was Friday. That meant he had to go to lunch with Millie.

"Come over here, boy." Nautica bit her bottom lip and signaled him with her index finger.

Tical walked over and stood in front of her, his manhood eye level with her. She took him into her warm mouth and purposely let her saliva drip while sucking him.

Tical wanted to stop her, but he couldn't. It felt too good. Every time he opened his mouth to tell Nautica he had to go, she seemed to hit the right spot with her tongue.

Loon called Nautica from his bedroom, so Millie wouldn't hear his conversation. He held his cell phone to his ear, only to get sent straight to voice mail. "Bitch!" He redialed the number and still got no response. The Patrón shots had him hard as a missile. He had to get another piece of her. He decided to leave a message:

Listen, bitch, first of all, never send me to voice mail again. Second, I'm trying to see you as soon as possible. You better call me back, or I'ma be upset. No, fuck it, I'm not going to get upset. Maybe I will just send this little tape I got to Tical or maybe even FedEx it to the Flint police department. Ha, ha, ha! Nautica, call me back. He pushed the end button.

He pulled out a gram of coke and made a line on the table.

Millie finished rubber-banding the last stack. Ready to go, she yelled to the back, "What taking you so long back there, nigga?" Her feelings were hurt because Tical had rescheduled lunch. They'd never missed a Friday. "I know it's that bitch in his ear," she mumbled.

"What you back there doing? Shitting? Hurry up!"

Millie grabbed the remote and clicked on the TV while waiting for Loon to return, so he could drop her back off to her car on the block. When she clicked on the TV, she accidentally pushed the play button connected to the VCR, and what she saw blew her mind. It was a homemade tape of two women naked on the bed in a sixty-nine position.

She walked over to the television and confirmed the face. "What daf!" She couldn't believe her eyes. "What the fuck is Loon doing with this?" she whispered. She took the tape out of the VCR. She couldn't wait to show Tical what his girl had been up to.

HOOD RAT

Chapter Twenty-five

Millie sped to Tical's house to break the news to him. *I knew that bitch was grimy! I knew it! Can't wait to tell Tical about his hood rat-ass ho.* She couldn't understand how Loon got the tape, but she didn't care. She dialed Tical's number over and over, getting voice mail every time.

After a couple minutes, she was pulling into his driveway and hopped out with the tape in hand. She used her key to get into the house. "Tical! Tical!"

Nautica heard Millie's voice as she stepped out of the shower. *What the fuck is she doing here?* She grabbed her terry-cloth robe and wrapped herself in it. *Tical must've came back.*

"Tical?" Nautica yelled as she made her way down the stairs. That's when she saw Millie standing with something in one hand, and the other hand on her hip. "Tical's not here, Millie," she said with a heavy attitude, knowing Tical had told her about popping in without knocking or ringing the doorbell.

"Bitch, shut the fuck up!" she yelled, trying to see, was he in the house. Tical!"

"Didn't you hear me the first time, Millie? He . . . is . . . not . . . here," she said, emphasizing every word.

"You dirty-ass bitch. I knew you wasn't all what you put on to be." Millie waved the tape in the air.

Nautica already knew what it was.

"Yeah, bitch, you ain't talking all that shit anymore, huh? You dirty-ass ho. I watched the rest of it and saw what you and your friend did. Robbing niggas and shit. I can't wait to show Tical this, so he can kick yo' ass to the curb. One thing Tical hates is a liar. I saw him kill his own cousin because he lied to him, so think about what he would do to yo' hood rat ass."

"Look, Millie, it's not what you think," Nautica said in a pleading tone.

"Bitch, you don't have to explain nothing to me." Millie picked up her phone to try Tical again.

Nautica lunged at her, wrestling her to the ground, and began to swing on her wildly, totally taking Millie off guard. She grabbed the lamp from the stand and smashed it against Millie's head, causing her to release the tape.

Nautica grabbed the tape and stood up. As Millie shook her head, trying to shake off the stars she was seeing, she ran to the kitchen for a hammer and smashed the tape into little pieces.

When she turned around, Millie walked in with her gun pointed at her. "You got a good one on me."

"Look, Millie, I love Tical and I can't jeopardize what we have,"

"Love and lies can't co-exist. I just want Tical to be happy. That's all I ever wanted. But it's women like you who corrupt good men. Bitches like you make men say a female ain't nothing but a ho or trick. I knew it was something about you, I just couldn't put my finger on it."

Humbled, Nautica looked down the barrel of the gun. "So you're going to kill me?"

"You're not even worth the bullet. I'm just going to let Tical know about the *real* you." Millie lowered her gun and looked at Nautica as if she was the scum of the earth. She walked out, leaving Nautica standing there feeling stupid.

Nautica knew that, with no tape, it was her word against Millie's, so she had to turn Tical against Millie before Millie got a chance to talk to him. Little did she know, Millie thought one step ahead, just like Tical had taught her to. She'd made a copy of the tape.

TICAL'S PLIGHT

Chapter Twenty-six

How could she talk to me like that? Tical was standing in his office looking at the construction crew upgrade his already immaculate club. She not only hurt his heart, she hurt his pride by talking to him like he wasn't boss. His sweet li'l Millie wasn't so sweet anymore. It seemed like she had a grudge against him. *I'ma have to show her ass some tough love.* His phone began to vibrate. It was Millie.

"Hello."

"Oh my goodness, Tical! I'm glad you picked up," Millie said in a rushed breath.

"What do you want, Millian?"

"It's about that bitch Nautica! I got—"

"Look! You're going to have to respect my woman. I'm tired of you coming at me all sideways. If it was any other mu'fucka talkin' to me like that they'd be circled in chalk right now. You act like I'm fucking you or something!"

Millie couldn't believe Tical's tone. She hung up on him, leaving him talking to a dial tone. Her hero had just made her feel so small, she was devastated. She buried her head in the wheel and cried her eyes out.

Tical couldn't believe Millie had hung up in his face. He felt his phone vibrate and thought Millie was calling back, but it was Nautica that time.

Nautica had to think fast. When she'd called Loon and asked him why did he break the agreement, he told her that Millie had stolen the tape.

Nautica suddenly got an idea. She ran upstairs, pulled down the Bob Marley portrait, and began to open Tical's safe. She had peeped the combination, which Tical thought only he and Millie knew. She grabbed one of his duffle bags and filled it with money.

After minutes of stuffing the bag, she put on some clothes and rushed downstairs. She picked up the phone to call Loon.

REGRETS

Chapter Twenty-seven

Nautica met up with Loon at a park on the outskirts of Baltimore. She walked toward him with a duffle bag full of money as he waited for her on the park bench. She walked over and dropped the bag at his feet.

Loon looked at the bag. "What's this?"

"That's just under one hundred thousand." Nautica, big shades and scarf draped over her head, only exposing her face, looked around to see if anyone was watching.

"For what?" He opened the bag and peeked in.

"I want to end this little thing you got over me, understand? It's going too far."

Loon looked at her toned legs, and it only enticed him more. He wasn't going to give that up for any amount of money. Nautica didn't understand, it was never about the money or sex. Loon wanted the power, and the baddest chick on his arm, something he dreamed about coming up.

"You uptight because Millie saw the tape, huh?" Loon smiled and touched Nautica's legs.

Nautica pulled away. "Yeah. How did she get the damn tape anyway?"

"I didn't give it to her. She just took it when she was over, counting money with me." Loon kept smiling, as if it was all just a big game to him.

"Look, Loon, are you going to take the money or what?" Nautica asked, tired of beating around the bush. "And there is another part of the deal, too."

"What's that?"

"You have to take the money and move out of town. It has to be over, Loon. It has to stop now!" Nautica glanced around again.

"Yeah, I'm going to take the money." Loon stood up and picked up the bag. "But I ain't going nowhere! I want to taste you tonight. Meet me at my spot later," he said, just before he walked off, leaving Nautica standing there dumbfounded.

Although Loon didn't accept her offer, his taking the money still played an integral part in her plan to turn Tical against Millie.

She picked up her phone and dialed Tical's number.

"Hello."

Nautica yelled into the phone, "Baby! Oh my God!," and put on a crying act.

"Calm down, Nautica. What's wrong?"

"Millie! She just ran in the house and hit me over the head with the gun. Baby, she was about to kill me!" Nautica sobbed loudly.

"What?!"

"Millie! She ran in the house and stole all of your money out of the safe. She told me that you were going to die and she was the one that got Church to try to kill you." Nautica was making up the story as she went on. "She was jealous of us being together. I never saw her like that, Tical. She was acting crazy as hell!"

"What?" Tical whispered.

"It was her all along. I'm worried, Tical. She might come back here."

Tical hung up the phone and dropped to his knees in the middle of his office. He'd just lost his other half in Millie. "Why, Millie, why?" he whispered, and buried his face in his hands.

Tical sat in his den with Gunplay and Nautica, and Gunplay was questioning her about Millie's actions.

"So you're saying she just came in and hit you with the gun?"

Nautica, in fake tears, nodded her head.

"And she said she sent Church to kill Tical?"

"I told you a million times. Yes!" Nautica broke down and began to cry hysterically.

Gunplay had his phone out, trying to dial Millie, but she kept sending him to voice mail. He just couldn't believe Millie would rob Tical.

"That's enough." Tical got up and walked over to Nautica. He ran his fingers through her hair "Go on upstairs, baby."

Nautica pecked Tical on the lips and headed upstairs.

"She has been acting different lately." Tical paced the room.

Gunplay looked up at Tical. "Yeah, I have been noticing it too. But I didn't think it was like this. I been blowing up her phone, and she won't even pick up."

"She won't for me either. She let jealousy come before family. Family comes first!" Tical yelled.

"You think she went back to the drugs?" Gunplay asked, not seeing any other explanation

"Seems like it."

Tical had always told himself and Millie that he would kill her before he let her kill herself slowly with heroin. He stopped pacing, knowing that what he was about to say would hurt, but it had to be done. He'd always taught Millie to aim for the number one spot. He believed that his own teachings came back to bite him.

But he also taught her to have no mercy when someone crosses the family. "Make it quick and painless," he said as he walked over to the bar and poured himself a drink.

"What?" Gunplay stood up.

"You heard me!" He yelled. "Don't make this anymore hurtful than it already is." He slammed the glass on the bar.

"Okay, Tical, okay." Gunplay held down his head and walked out of the den.

Tical dropped a tear, his bottom lip quivering, and his hand bleeding from the broken glass.

Millie cried as she packed up her belongings in her apartment and prepared to leave the city. She didn't know where she was going, but she had to get away from Baltimore. She grabbed the picture of her and Tical and traced the outline of his face with her index finger. "I love you," she said. She put it in her suitcase.

She walked over to her table and picked up the letter she'd just written to him. She put everything that she wanted to say to him in there. She kissed it and sat it on top of a cigar box she wanted him to have.

Millie picked up the suitcase and headed for the door. She was going to leave B-more and let Tical enjoy his happiness. As she walked toward the door, she saw that someone was turning her knob and coming in.

"What the—"She grabbed her gun from her ankle holster and watched as the man exposed himself. "Oh, Gunplay! You scared me." She tossed her gun on the couch.

Gunplay remained silent as he walked in, never taking his eye off her.

She saw Gunplay's watery eyes. "Nigga, what's wrong with you?" And the next thing she saw after that was the barrel of his gun.

Gunplay walked out of Millie's apartment with a smoking gun and tears in his eyes. He punched his fist through the wall in the hallway. He couldn't believe what he'd just done. He called Tical and waited for him to pick up. "I did it. She's gone, Tical. She's gone," he murmured.

"Okay, Gunplay. Call the cleaners." Tical hung up.

Both men had a part of their heart gone with the loss of Millie, but it was all in the game. Millie broke the rules, so she had to deal with the consequences. Tical knew that if Millie tried to have him killed once, she would eventually do it again.

GUESS WHO'S COMING TO DINNER?

Chapter Twenty-eight

Six Months Later

Tical had called a meeting for all his soldiers, telling them that the day had come when he was getting out of the game for real this time. There were new faces around the table, along with the old crew. He was finally ready to give up the game and start his life with Nautica. It was Friday evening, and about two hours before the scheduled dinner at Tical's retirement get-together. He puffed on a spliff while sitting in the den and playing chess with Gunplay Murdock.

"Yo, Tical, you really are walking away from this shit, huh?" Murdock, his eyes on the chessboard, moved his bishop.

Tical slowly blew out smoke from the corner of his mouth. "Yeah, bruh, I'm done with this game. If I stayed any longer, I would just be getting greedy. I have the residuals from the HBO show coming in, and I have a nice piece of change to start a new business venture, a legit one. The club is doing good. I can't ask for much more, right? I also have a beautiful woman that I want to spend the rest of my life with, ya dig. That's my heart right there." He glanced at the kitchen, where Nautica was preparing a meal for his inner circle. "What more can I ask for at twenty-eight?"

"You right. The smart ones get out the game at the right time."

Murdock was smiling on the inside. It was his time to become the head guy of the operation, but he was going to miss hustling with his best friend. He also had an empty spot in his heart for Millie.

Tical looked around and then leaned over the table, so that only Murdock could hear him. "Yo, I got something to show you."

Looking over his shoulder again to make sure the coast was clear, he reached into his pocket and pulled out a small black box. He popped it open and revealed the luminous diamond that sat on a platinum band. The diamond was humongous and sparkled as the light hit it.

He whispered, "I'ma ask Nautica to marry me tonight."

Murdock was skeptical. He thought back to the time he'd seen Nautica and Loon coming from the bottom deck on Tical's yacht. He wanted to tell him that he should fall back and make sure she was the one for him before he popped the question, but when he saw the look in Tical's eyes, he didn't want to steal his man's happiness.

"Congratulations, man! She's going to make a beautiful wife." Murdock reached over the table to give him a pound.

Tical smiled, knowing that he had his man's blessing. He was more excited than a young child. He was the happiest man on earth. He put the box in his pocket and concentrated on the chess game.

Nautica swung around the kitchen counter to check the lamb chops. She peeked in the oven and everything was coming along fine. She stirred the sides that she cooked on the stovetop. She reached into the second oven to take out the biscuits and accidentally dropped the tray on the floor. She was antsy with the thought of Loon coming over for dinner. He hadn't been around lately and hadn't asked for any sexual favors since Millie's death, but Nautica still was on edge when around him.

"Damn!" She bent over to pick the tray and food from the floor and felt a hand touch her behind.

"Hey, baby." Tical gently grabbed her waist. "Everything okay? You seem uptight."

"Ooh! You scared me. Yeah, I'm okay." She felt Tical's manhood against her behind.

Tical gently stood her up and began to kiss the nape of her neck, and Nautica closed her eyes in complete pleasure, her body tingling at his touch. She felt his hand slip under her dress. She never wore panties, so Tical had easy access to her love box.

"Wait, wait. Murdock is in the next room, and people are going to be coming any minute now," she whispered as she continued to rub him passionately.

"I sent Gunplay out for champagne, and we have about a half an hour before anyone is supposed to show up." Tical licked his fingertips and began to gently stroke Nautica's clitoris in circular motions, all the while looking into her eyes.

Nautica began to moan. She placed one of her legs on the counter for a better angle.

Tical couldn't take any more of the foreplay. He scooped her up by her plump buttocks and sat her on the counter. He quickly dropped his pants and boxers and slid in, as Nautica sucked his neck and rubbed his back. He let out a quiet grunt as he felt her warmth.

"Ooh, baby, I love you." Nautica wrapped both of her arms around him tight and held on as if she was on a roller-coaster.

Tical went as deep as he could and rotated his hips in loops. He didn't go in and out, he just moved in circles, touching her back walls, and his pelvis was rubbing her clitoris, making it swollen. That drove Nautica insane, and she moaned loudly and dug her nails into his back.

Tical began to go up and down, lifting Nautica up off the counter every time he went up. The sound of Nautica's behind slapping against the counter only enticed him more. He sped up at her request, feeling himself about to have an orgasm.

Nautica also was on the verge of cumming. She thrust her midsection against Tical, and before long, he let out a roar as he pulled out and released himself on the floor. He continued to rub Nautica's clitoris, and seconds later a small squirt came from her love box. Her legs began to shake vigorously, and she gripped him tight. They'd only had sex for five minutes, but both of them had great climaxes.

Nautica hopped off the counter and straightened herself up as she heard the door open. Tical pulled up his pants and winked at his woman, letting her know the sex was good.

"You're so bad." She quickly grabbed a napkin and began to look for Tical's semen. "Where is it at?" She looked down at the floor and counter. They searched the kitchen for Tical's seeds, but there was no sign of it.

"I must've shot a blank."

They both laughed. Tical grabbed her around the waist, and they both began to stare into each other's eyes, smiling.

Gunplay Murdock returned from his run. He walked in with two bottles of Chandon. "Yo, get a room," he said playfully. He stuck the bottles in the freezer.

"Too late," Tical whispered in Nautica's ear.

They both giggled.

Nautica looked up and saw Loon standing in the doorway of the kitchen.

Tical felt her body tense up and he looked back to see what was wrong. He saw Loon standing there with a slight smile.

"What's good, Tical?" Loon said as a smile spread. He walked over to Tical with an open hand.

"What's up, Loon? I didn't know you were here." Tical slapped hands with Loon, and they halfway hugged, bumping shoulders.

"I walked in with Gunplay." Loon focused his attention on Nautica. "Hello, miss. It's a pleasure seeing you again." He scooped up her hand and attempted to kiss it.

Nautica snatched her hand away from him. The very sight of him made her want to vomit.

"Fuck you doing, li'l nigga?" Tical said playfully. "Ol' 'Rico Suave'-ass nigga." He shook his head.

Tical and Murdock laughed at the young'un trying to be smooth, but little did they know, he'd sexed Nautica on many occasions.

"Okay, I'ma let you get back to work, baby. I have to holla at these niggas before everyone arrives." Tical tapped Nautica on the butt and headed out of the kitchen.

Loon and Murdock followed Tical, Loon being the last one to exit. He looked at Nautica, who was staring at him with pure hatred.

"Oh yeah, baby, I forgot to give you something," Loon said in a low tone as he reached into his pants pocket and pulled out a folded piece of paper and tossed it to her.

Nautica caught it. "What the fuck is wrong with you, crazy mu'fucka?" she whispered. "Won't you just leave me alone, you bitch-ass nigga?"

"You need to read that, and if you don't play my game by my rules, I'ma spill the beans before the main course. Understand me?"

A deranged smile on his face, Loon was having more fun torturing Nautica than he ever had in his entire life. He walked out to join his boss, leaving Nautica in the kitchen alone with his note.

Nautica opened the letter. *I can't handle this shit. That nigga is a psycho. I have to do something to stop this!*

"So you are going to hand over everything?" Murdock sipped on the Chandon.

Tical sat at the head of the table, his hands folded. He observed his eight most loyal soldiers. He took a sip of his Rémy Martin and took his time before he answered, as he always did, choosing every single word he spoke carefully. He looked at the empty chair next to Gunplay and thought about Millie's betrayal. He clenched his jaws and remained silent as he had images of Millie and her beautiful smile. A wave of guilt overcame him. He shook his head slowly, thinking about his Millie.

He snapped out of his daze and looked directly at Murdock. "Yeah, I'm going to introduce you to the connect in the upcoming weeks. We're going to take a trip to LA and get you associated. I'm giving you the keys to the world, Gunplay. I know you're capable of taking over and running a smooth operation, and now it's your time. The game will be good to you, if you are good to it."

Tical then looked at Loon and gave him a rare grin. "Loon, you have a heart of a warrior, ya dig. I never saw a nigga like you. You get busy. But the murder game days are over for you. You put in work, and now it's time for you to move up, understand? A man is only as strong as his right hand. Gunplay was my right hand for years, and I never fell, because he was my crutch. It's your turn to become Gunplay's crutch and move up in the ranks and start dealing with weight."

Loon's eyes lit up. He'd been waiting for an opportunity like this since he first got into the street life. He had already thought about the way he'd play his position. He'd wait for the perfect time to cross Gunplay, so that he'd be the number one man. In his twisted mind he'd decided that Gunplay would die.

"I'm ready," he said, nodding his head up and down.

The other soldiers sat at the table and listened closely as Tical passed the game down to them and gave them all the knowledge that he had. Everyone felt odd because of the absence of Millie. They knew she would've been the candidate for the right hand, if she hadn't met her untimely death. Most of the soldiers at the table didn't care for Loon and hated his whole style, not to mention, he was the youngest at the table.

"This is to the good life." Tical raised his glass, and everyone followed suit and held up their glasses for the toast.

Just then Nautica walked in with two dinner dishes and placed them on the center of the table. She had on her cooking apron and red high heels, the pair that Loon demanded she wear in the letter he gave her in the kitchen. And there were other demands too.

"Hey, baby, I'm starving," Tical said.

Nautica tried to hurry out.

"Take a seat and sit down and eat with us. We are done talking business." Tical pulled a chair out next to him.

Nautica's palms began to sweat. She didn't want Tical to notice her uneasiness. She hesitantly sat down and watched the men dig into the food. She glanced over at Loon and he looked at her with a menacing smirk while staring at her. She couldn't believe the request in the letter he had. She was sweating bullets as she felt like her heart was in her throat.

Tical noticed how much she was sweating, something rare with her. "You okay, ma?" Tical whispered as he leaned closer to her and rubbed her thigh.

Nautica quickly tried to act normal as she put on a fake smile and placed her sweaty hand on

top of Tical's. "I'm okay. Just don't feel so good."
She leaned over and pecked him on the cheek.

"Could you pass me the salt?" Loon smiled
and reached out his hand.

Nautica shot a cold stare at Loon, and if looks
could kill, he would've been in a body bag. Searching for anything to excuse herself from the table,
Nautica quickly stood up and said, "Oh, I forgot to
set out the biscuits," and returned to the kitchen.

Lightheaded and breathing heavily, Nautica
rested both of her hands on the kitchen counter.
Her hatred for Loon was at an all-time high.

She began to put the biscuits in the basket, so
she could return to the table. *I hate this nigga.
Something's gotta give. I have to tell Tical. But
will he forgive me? If I tell him about everything, will he leave me, like everyone else in
my life?* Nautica thought about she being the
reason Millie got murdered. She didn't think Tical would take it that far. *If he did that to Millie,
what would he do to me if he found out I lied
about seeing her taking the money? I can't lose
Tical, he's all I have.*

She quickly wiped away the tears and finished
loading the bread basket with the new biscuits
she'd baked. She rubbed her hands through her
hair, exhaled deeply, and scooped up the basket.
Just as she was about to exit the kitchen, she

noticed a biscuit on the floor with what looked like a clear gel on top of it. She instantly began to smile, knowing she'd found Tical's sperm from their quickie. She bent down and picked it up especially for Loon. She reached in the refrigerator and grabbed the spray butter to disguise Loon's little surprise. She sprayed the butter over all the biscuits, extra on Loon's, and placed his biscuit on top, in plain sight, so she wouldn't get it mixed up with the others.

Nautica returned to the dining area with the basket. She took her tongs and walked around the table, placing a biscuit on each man's plate. She took the biscuit with the "extra sauce" and placed it on Loon's plate and returned to her seat, smiling like the happiest woman on earth.

"My baby makes the best biscuits," Tical said as he dug into his food.

Gunplay took a bite of the biscuit. "Yeah, Nautica can throw down in the kitchen."

"Yeah, you knows how I do," Nautica said playfully, fixing her own plate. "Loon, dig in." She tried her best not to burst out into laughter. She sneakily watched as Loon took a bite out of the biscuit, savored the taste, and gobbled up Tical's unborn children. *Now that's entertainment*, she thought.

Loon saw that Nautica was almost finished with her dinner. He thought it was the perfect time to have a little fun. He picked up his napkin and wiped his mouth. He then crossed his hands and wiped his eyebrow. He then shot a look at Nautica, who wasn't paying attention to him. *Oh, I see this bitch thinks it's a game.* He cleared his throat loudly to get her attention.

Everyone at the table was in deep conversation and didn't think anything of Loon clearing his throat, but Nautica knew what was up. He cleared his throat and glanced at Nautica again. When Nautica returned the glance, Loon wiped his eyebrow once again.

"Ruff!" Nautica barked loudly.

Loon had instructed her in the note to bark every time he wiped his eyebrow. He wiped his eyebrow again, this time trying not to laugh.

"Ruff!"

Tical, high from all the champagne and Rémy he'd downed throughout the night, was noticeably tipsy. "What's wrong with you?" he asked, thinking she had sneezed or something. He knew his woman hadn't just barked like a damn dog.

"Yeah, I'm okay. I just don't feel so good." She quickly rose up and stormed out of the dining area.

Everyone at the table ceased their conversations and looked around to see what was going on.

Nautica was so humiliated, she wanted to crawl under a rock and die. She rushed upstairs and flopped in her bed, while crying her eyes out.

Minutes later, Tical entered the room and sat on the bed next to his crying woman. "What's wrong, baby? Is everything okay?" he asked, swaying back and forth from the effects of the liquor.

"Yeah, I'm okay. I think I got a stomach flu or something. My tummy hurts so bad."

He stroked her back. *I know I'm kinda drunk, but sound like my baby was barking. Maybe she sneezed.* "Baby, I'm not trying to spring anything on you, but I have to go on a little business trip this weekend. Gunplay and I are leaving in two days. I was going to tell you after dinner, but I guess now is as good as it's gon' get."

Nautica sat up, holding her stomach. "On a trip?"

"Yeah. Remember the business associate I told you about in California?"

"Yeah, I remember."

"Well, he has his eyes on a new computer company that created a product that I'm interested in. It's a new computer system that I think I'm going to invest in. They're having a presentation for me and five other potential investors. I think it's going to be something big. I want to jump on board early."

"You have to go all the way to California again? Can I go with you?"

"You know better than that, baby. I don't want to bring you along on a business trip. Besides, you aren't feeling too well, and I don't want you to give me what you have when I have to do business. *And* it's a five-hour flight. You just stay home and wait for me, beautiful. When I return, we'll start looking for places in Miami." Tical kissed her on her forehead.

Nautica lit up at the sound of *Miami.* He was finally ready to move and get away from his fast life. She caught herself smiling too big, and grimaced as if her stomach was paining her. "I'm so glad we're leaving here and going to start our life together." She lay back down. *Finally I will be away from Loon, and my man and I can start our life together.*

Tical felt the box that held the engagement ring he was going to present to Nautica, but decided he'd wait until he returned from his trip to pop the question.

I love this girl. He rubbed her stomach. In his eyes, even balled-up sick, she was the most beautiful woman in the world. "I love you," he whispered. Then he pulled the cover over her and kissed her softly.

FAITHFUL

Chapter Twenty-nine

The beams from the morning sun peeked through the blinds, waking Nautica from her peaceful slumber. She slowly rolled over and felt for Tical as she did every morning, but his side of the bed was cold. That startled her. Then she remembered he went out of the state for a couple of days.

Nautica sat up and wiped the sleep out of her eye and stretched her arms over her head, releasing the tension from her upper body. She stepped out of the bed, completely naked, and walked over to the blinds to let the sun light up the dim room. She looked over at the empty bed and realized how long it had been since she woke up alone. *I miss you already, Tical.* She picked the remote up from the night-stand and pointed it toward the surround sound system. She turned it to disc five, her favorite CD, *The Miseducation of Lauryn Hill*, and turned it to track three.

She walked into the bathroom to take a hot shower, but before she reached the bathroom the sound of the doorbell echoed throughout the house. "Who the fuck is that ringing the bell this early?" she said to herself. She grabbed her all-white terrycloth robe and quickly threw it on. She walked down the stairs, tying the robe up across her waist.

The doorbells continued to chime, but at a more rapid pace. *Ding-dong! Ding-dong!*

"Hold up, damn! I'm coming!" Nautica hurried down the porcelain stairs and approached the door. She unlocked the deadbolt and opened the big oak cherry door.

"Good morning, baby," Loon said, expressionless.

Nautica covered herself, closing the top part of her robe and depriving Loon of any visual pleasure. She didn't know what to say to his crazed ass. She didn't think he'd have the guts to come to the house in Tical's absence. "What the fuck are you doing here, Loon? Are you out of your fuckin' mind? Huh?"

"You know why I'm here, baby. Stop playing." Loon licked his lips, and his eyes drifted to her midsection, where the robe hugged her curves.

"Look, Loon, you can't do this. You have to leave!" she yelled.

Nautica attempted to close the door in his face, but Loon put his boot in the door and pushed it back open. "No, bitch, you listen to me! I can do what the fuck I want to do. You already know the deal! Betta get with the program, baby!" He reached for her robe and untied it.

Nautica watched helplessly as Loon stood in the doorway and degraded her. He opened her robe completely, exposing her supple breasts and neatly shaved vagina. He grabbed her breasts and walked up on her, his stink breath creeping into her nostrils.

She cringed at his touch. "You a foul nigga, Loon. You foul as hell."

Loon bent down and began to suck her nipple, slowly edging her inside the house and closing the door behind him. He dropped to his knees in front of her. A single tear slid down Nautica's face as she reluctantly spread her legs for Loon to give her oral sex.

After Loon sloppily got her to the moistness, he forced her up the stairs and into the bedroom that overlooked the ocean. He took off his shirt and walked over to the gigantic window to enjoy the view. The feeling of power overcame him as he stood in the shoes of a boss for a brief second. *So this how it feels?* he thought, as he momentarily fulfilled his childhood dream to be the dopeman.

He gripped the back of Nautica's neck and forced her to look toward the window and into the beautiful ocean front. "Isn't this beautiful?" He looked back at her, tears streaming from her eyes as she stood naked with her legs crossed tight.

Loon slid his tongue into her mouth while groping her entire body. He dropped his pants and unveiled his erection. He turned her around, so that he was behind her, and pushed her to the window. He wanted to make love to her while she viewed the ocean.

Nautica's reluctantly placed her hands on the window. She knew she had to play by his rules. "I hate you," she whispered as he entered her soaked wound. She decided that the only way to stop Loon was to tell Tical the truth, or kill him.

Tical's breath became shallow as he and Murdock looked through high-powered binoculars and witnessed Loon sex his woman. He was stationed in a speedboat on the ocean. He threw the binoculars down in rage and shook his head and he puffed on a spliff. He inhaled deeply as he stared into the clouds. He'd had suspicions of Nautica's infidelity, but his love for her gave her the benefit of the doubt. The brief business trip to California was a total falsehood, just so he could see if his uncertainties were true. Not only was she cheating, but she was sexing one of his workers, the ultimate disrespect. Tical was speechless as he blew the smoke out, his pain hidden behind dark Cavalli shades. Gunplay placed his hand on Tical's shoulder. "I knew she was grimy."

Tical puffed away in silence. He looked at the cigar box he'd found in Millie's apartment days after he sent Murdock over to handle her, and only just recently had the courage to open. He thought about what he'd found in it the night before. It broke his heart to see Nautica having a ménage à trois on tape. He'd also witnessed her friend shoot one of his old buyers. He was totally shocked to see what type of person Nautica was.

He picked up the folded piece of paper out of the box and re-read it.

Tical,

I could never tell you this face to face, because I couldn't stand to see your eyes when you found out the truth. I see the way you look at Nautica and I never saw you light up about anything or anyone like you did when her name was mentioned. A deep part of me inside wants you to look that way when you view me. I want you to look at me like you look at her, with love. Tical, I admire you and the strong man that you are. You cared about me when no one on this earth gave a damn. Although you are not much older than me , you are the only father I ever known. Although you never made love to me physically, over the past years you have made love to my mind and you had my heart from the start. To be honest with you, I wish I was Nautica, to be the one under you at night and kissing you in the morning. I know you could never look at me in that way, so I've made a decision to leave town and let you be happy. My jealousy would only cause misery to your relationship, and I owe you much more than that. The only thing I want is for you to be happy and I see that she brings you joy, so I'm glad for you. If I have never told you this, I love you, Tical, and I will always be your girl.

Before I leave, I do want you to check something out. Something was brought to my attention, and I just want you to know the whole truth about Nautica. Not to try to sabotage your relationship, but I think you deserve to know the real truth about her. I want you to watch the video I sent

*with this note, and before you judge her,
please remember that everyone has a past
and anyone can change. I remember when
you told me that when you found me at
that truck stop. You changed my life and
made me into a woman, and I hope you
can do the same for her. No one loves you
more than me. And no one ever will. I love
you.*

Your girl, Millie

Tical began to question his order to end Millie's life. Nautica was the one who convinced me that she wasn't loyal. I can't believe this.

"So do you want me to handle that for you?" Gunplay asked, knowing how Tical got down. He'd already thought about tying both of them up and killing them together. But he would kill Loon first, so Nautica could witness the demise of her undercover lover.

"What?" Tical snatched the shades off his face, revealing his red eyes. Although he had just discovered his woman's infidelities and past life, he still loved her, and was more disappointed than upset with her. He wanted to make things right and just bring his woman closer to him. Millie's note told him that anyone could change, a phrase that kept replaying in his head. "I want you to take care of Loon. Fix him up real nice for me." He tossed the butt of the spliff into the ocean.

"And what about Nautica?"

"I'm going to ask her one time, one more time." Tical put up his index finger, tears welling up in his eyes. "And if she tells me the truth, I'ma let her breathe. I ain't gon' front, man, I love that girl; she's my other half. But if she lies to me, I want you to take care of her. Understand?" He curled his finger as if he was pulling a trigger.

"Understood." Gunplay had never seen Tical so emotional, so it told him how much he really cared for Nautica.

GUNPLAY & CONFESSIONS

Chapter Thirty

Nautica scrubbed herself vigorously in the shower while crying a river. She was trying so desperately to wash Loon's scent from her body. The shower had run cold because she had been in it for two and a half hours trying to wash all of the guilt away. But it didn't work out because, when she stepped out, the pain was still on her shoulders.

She dried off and walked into the bedroom. *I can't do this shit anymore. I'm going to have to tell Tical the truth!* She picked up her cell phone and dialed Tical's number. It sent her straight to voice mail. She heard the beep and tried to confess, but the only words that came out of her mouth were, "I love you, Tical. I can't wait for you to come home to me." She couldn't bring herself to tell him.

She flipped down her phone and tossed it on the bed. She'd made the decision right there that she would never lie to Tical again. She reached under the mattress and pulled out the small .22 caliber pistol that he kept under his bed and held it in her hand. She would kill Loon and end this nightmare.

Nautica picked up the phone and dialed Loon's number.

"Yo."

"Hey, daddy! I can't help myself. I want you again."

"I knew you were going to come around. You want some more of this good dick, don't you?" Loon grabbed himself. Nautica had finally come to her senses and realized how much he loved and admired her.

"I want it so bad, I'm so wet. It's running down my leg."

"Enough said! Daddy is on his way."

"No!" Nautica yelled when she caught herself. She wanted to kill him inside of his own home. "I want to fuck you in your bed, where we belong," she said in the sexiest voice she could muster. "I'm on my way right now. I won't have anything on but my pumps and a trench coat. Please be naked and hard when I come in. I can't wait to feel you inside of me again."

"Hurry up, baby. I got something fo' that ass!"

"I can't come right now. Let's meet up later tonight."

"Cool. Come through around eight."

Nautica hung up the phone and inhaled deeply, her hands shaking. She rushed to her closet and pulled out the leather trench coat Tical had purchased her for her birthday. She laid the coat on the bed, along with the gun, and began to plot. She could hardly wait until later that night to put all of the drama to rest with one bullet.

The sun was just setting on the purple-hued clouds when Nautica arrived at Loon's small house in the inner city of Baltimore. She pulled her Range Rover to the side and checked her rearview mirrors to make sure no one was watching her. The streets were empty, except for a couple of raggedy cars parked on the curb. She secured her gun in her thigh-high stocking and exited the car, looking around through her shaded glasses.

All of her limbs trembled as she made her way to his porch. The closer she got to the house, the clearer she heard the sounds of Bob Marley blasting. She approached the door and knocked. *Tap, tap, tap!* The music was so loud, she was sure Loon wouldn't be able to hear her. She placed her hand on the doorknob and turned. To her surprise, it was already open.

She slowly pushed the door wide open and crept in. The smell of incense filled the air, and red and white rose petals trailed from the front door to the back. *This nigga is crazy. He really think I fell for him.* She pulled out her gun from her stockings and followed the trail of petals. The music grew louder and louder as she approached the back bedroom, where flickering candles barely illuminated the room.

Nautica crept into the room and saw the silhouette of Loon's naked body in the bed. She flipped the gun off safety and flipped on the light switch. What she saw made her drop her gun—Loon's bloody dead body was sprawled across the bed, his penis stuffed into his mouth.

Nautica's knees gave out on her, and she fell to the ground. The strong smell of blood disgusted her, and she vomited in her mouth. After regaining her poise, she picked up her gun to leave out. Just before closing his front door, she reached into her pocket and grabbed a handkerchief and wiped the door handle. Her hands were shaking so badly, she couldn't even wipe the door good.

She stormed off and got into her car and started the ignition. She hit the gas and the sound of screeching tires erupted as she exited the block. "What the fuck!" she yelled as she hopped on the expressway back home.

Nautica felt like a massive weight had been lifted from her shoulders. *I hope that mu'fucka died a slow death. I'm glad someone got his ass,* she thought as she sped home.

The sight of a dead body had her nerves bad, and she was shaking like a heroin addict. She pulled over to the side of the road to calm herself and rested her head on the steering wheel. She took a long deep breath, glad the blackmailing and torture was over.

Gunplay and Tical watched Nautica run out of Loon's home as they sat in the beat-up Grand Am. He'd instructed Murdock to get a less noticeable car, so they wouldn't stick out like a sore thumb in the run-down neighborhood. He noticed that she was wearing pumps and a long leather coat that he had purchased her, which made his blood boil even more. He knew she was naked under the coat. He shook his head from side to side when she sped right past them. *Why, baby? Why, beautiful? I loved you with all my heart, and this is how you repay me?* Tical's heart thumped, and his bottom lip quivered. He felt like a baboon was trying to get out of his chest, but his pride made him hold back the tears.

Gunplay was wiping Loon's blood from his hands and face as he looked on with Tical. Loon's death had been a messy one.

Tical had found close to $200,000 dollars in Loon's closet and instantly knew it was the money he'd stolen from the safe, because of the position of the bills. Tical always folded his money face upward. At that moment he knew Millie wasn't the one who did it, and he was consumed with guilt. He figured that Loon and Nautica had been plotting on him from the beginning and thought about them being from the same city, and the way Nautica acted nervous whenever Loon was around.

The two men remained silent, and Gunplay could see the hurt in his friend.

A rare tear almost slid down Tical's face, but he quickly wiped it away. He clenched his jaws and teeth, and his breathing became louder by the second. Tical then took one deep breath and exhaled slowly. "I'm going to ask her once; if she lies, you know what to do." Tical threw his head in the direction he wanted Murdock to drive, and Murdock pulled off.

When Tical and Gunplay reached the house, Tical noticed that Nautica hadn't made it there yet. *Where is she at?* he thought as they entered the house.

"Fuck it! Gunplay, you know the drill. If she denies it," Tical's voice cracked, "rock her to sleep." He walked to the bar and poured himself a glass of Rémy Martin.

At that moment, they heard the sound of keys jingling and the front door opening.

Nautica came in and locked the door, not even noticing that she wasn't alone. She turned around and jumped as she saw Tical standing before her. "Whew, Tical! You scared the mess out of me," she said, her hand on her chest.

Tical stood there with no emotion as he slowly shook the glass in a circular motion, clinking the ice together. He took a sip, staring at Nautica intently.

"I missed you! I thought you weren't coming home until Sunday?"

"Change of plans," Tical said coldly.

Nautica remembered she didn't have on anything under her jacket. *Aw shit! What the fuck am I going to do? I'm butt-ass naked under this jacket. Damn!* She tried to think of a way to squirm out of the situation. "Ooh, I have to pee, excuse me." She brushed past Tical and headed for the stairs. "Hey, Gunplay." She headed up the stairs, relieved that Tical didn't stop her. *That was close!*

"Yo, babygirl! Come here for a minute!" Tical walked to the bottom of the stairs. "I want to ask you something."

"Baby, I have to go! Can it just wait?" She squirmed as if she really had to use the restroom.

"I said come here!" Tical threw his glass against the wall, causing it to shatter.

Nautica flinched. "Baby, what's wrong? Is everything okay?" *Oh my God, he knows. He knows.* She slowly made her way down the stairs.

Tical quickly calmed himself and smiled. "Sorry, baby. I'm just so stressed out right now. I'm buggin." He rubbed his temples and shook his head from side to side, as if he was experiencing a bad migraine. He reached out and took her hand and led her to the couch, where they both sat down.

Gunplay Murdock immediately went to the den and out of sight.

"What's going on, baby?" Nautica asked nervously, trying her best to keep her jacket closed. She looked into Tical's eyes. She'd never seen such a sincere, loving look.

"Yeah, everything is okay." He gently kissed her hand and held it with both hands tightly. "Nautica, you know I care for you so much, and I want to spend the rest of my life with you. Since I met you, I have become a better man. What I'm trying to say is that you complete me, and it's me and you against the world. I will always love you, no matter what. I love you for the person you are, and I would never judge you. I love you unconditionally. That's my word." Tical paused and looked into her eyes.

"Tical, I love you too. You are my soul mate," she responded, becoming more comfortable.

"I want to ask you something, okay."

"Okay, baby, anything."

"Are you cheating on me, or have been?" Tical tried to study Nautica's eyes. He felt like a fool for even considering forgiving her and prayed silently that she would just come clean, so the rebuilding process could start.

Nautica thought long and hard. *Why is he asking? He has to know.* Nautica looked in Tical's eyes, and they were full of love and admiration. If Tical knew something, he'd be more upset. She decided to lie and promised herself it would be the last time she ever lied to him. "No, Tical. I never would do that. I know Millie had you thinking negative about me, but I am your woman, and I would never disrespect you. It's me and you against the world, remember?" She looked him directly into his eyes.

"Okay, okay." Tical gently patted her hands and leaned over to kiss her. A kiss of death. A tear rolled down his eye as his lips touched her soft skin, and he hugged her tight, so she wouldn't notice his misery.

He stood up and walked to the den to join Gunplay, never looking back at Nautica. He couldn't look at her because he knew what was about to happen. Those few steps were the hardest steps he'd even taken.

Nautica took a deep breath and thanked God that Tical didn't open up her jacket. She didn't want to risk going upstairs and have him follow her, only to discover she was naked underneath.

She quickly grabbed her keys and headed for the door. "Tical, I'll be right back. I'm about to pick up a few things from the mall," she yelled, not even waiting for a response.

Nautica planned on buying some clothes and putting them on before she returned and he would never know. She hopped in her car and sped off. She got about a block away from the condo and then made a complete stop. Shame plagued her. *That man is the only thing good that ever happened to me. I can't lie to him. I owe him so much more than that. I'm going to tell him the truth about everything, and if he truly loves me, he will accept who I was. I will tell him about Loon crazy ass and everything. I have to.* She made a U-turn back to the house.

As she pulled back into the driveway, Tical was on his way out. "Tical, I have to talk to you!" She got out of the car and ran to him.

Tical quickly moved her arm away from him and headed to the car. "I'll be right back. I have to make a run." He pushed the unlock button on his car and headed to it. He'd already given Gunplay the green light to kill her, instructing him to wait for her there and kill her when she returned home from the mall.

"Tical!" Nautica yelled.

Tical turned around.

"I love you." Nautica smiled. She felt so much better knowing she would tell him the whole truth and nothing but the truth.

Tical slowly nodded his head and got into his car. He watched as Nautica entered the house and wanted so badly to call for her, but he knew that once she crossed him things would never be the same. He sat in his car asking himself, *Why, Nautica, why?* He couldn't understand.

Just before he reached the end of the driveway, he heard a single shot coming from his condo. He knew Gunplay Murdock had put a slug through her head.

FOREVER

Chapter Thirty-one

Millie stared at the picture of her and Tical on her eighteenth birthday during the big bash he'd thrown for her. She cried as she stood in the window in her small apartment in New York City. She missed Tical so much, and although he'd ordered her murder, she still had respect and love for him.

Gunplay Murdock couldn't bring himself to kill her and had ordered her to leave town, telling her that, if he ever saw her in Baltimore, he wouldn't spare her life. Millie, hurt and confused, agreed to leave.

She gripped the picture and held it close to her chest as she stared into the projects playground where she'd spent a great part of her childhood.

Her body ached from the cravings of heroin, but she clenched her teeth and tightened her stomach as she fought through the pain. She would battle the withdrawal cold turkey, and when the day was right, she would return to Tical with a clean mind and soul. She even remembered Tical telling her that he would kill her before he saw her go through drug addiction again. Millie felt as if she was alone in the world, and the only friend she had was sitting on the counter and calling her name.

She glanced over at the heroin pack she had copped earlier and began to walk toward the table. The urge was too much for her to handle. She sat down in the kitchen chair, still holding the picture. She propped the picture up and stared at the photo. "I love you with all my heart, Tical. I'm so sorry," she whispered.

She began to melt the drug in a metal spoon, glancing back and forth from the picture to the syringe as she filled the needle with the narcotic. As she grabbed the belt that sat on the table and began to tie it around her forearm, she envisioned the old crew—herself, Gunplay Murdock, and Tical—and all of the good times they'd shared over the years.

Millie slowly inserted the needle in her swollen vein and relaxed as she felt the warm sensation creep up her arm. She slumped in the seat when the magic of the drug began to melt her pain away. She eased out of the chair and on to the floor, going in and out of her nod.

Nautica walked out of the bedroom and down the stairs. She couldn't believe she'd just killed Gunplay with a shot to his head. Before she'd shot him, he'd called her a lying, cheating bitch. She knew then that Tical had known about her lie that day. She walked at a snail's pace and flopped on the couch in total shock, gripping the .22 in her palm. She dropped the gun on the floor.

Nautica opened her jacket, exposing the bloody hole that rested in her stomach. The gunshot wound to her midsection was bleeding profusely, and she felt her life slipping away. She and Murdock had shot each other at the same time, but her bullet had killed him instantly.

Nautica wanted to die, because life was too hard and just too difficult to bear. She thought about Khia, and how she'd caused her death. And about Millie. She hated herself. She thought maybe it was God's way of punishing her for all that she had done. Slipping in and out of consciousness, she saw glimpses of her life, and then a bright light. But it wasn't the doors to heaven she was seeing. It was Tical coming through the front door in a frenzy.

He rushed to her and grabbed her limp body, tears pouring down his face. He cried like a baby as he saw his woman barely hold on to life. Blood trickled down the side of Nautica's mouth, and she appeared to force a smile as she looked into his eyes.

Tical's whispered, "I'm sorry. I'm so sorry, baby." He tried to put pressure on her wound, to stop the flow of blood.

Nautica tried to respond, but she couldn't. Her breath became shallow, and her heartbeat got slower, and slower, and slower. It was too late. God was calling her home.

Right at that moment, five masked men armed with automatic assault rifles ran into Tical's home. Then, a short, dark man with a cane and a slight limp came in.

Tical already knew the deal when he saw Black Pete, Church's father. He didn't even try to fight back or defend himself as the gunmen walked over to him, their guns drawn. He continued to cradle Nautica's lifeless body and rock her back and forth. He kissed her cheek and closed his eyes, prepared to meet her on the other side. "I love you, babygirl," he whispered.

Black Pete nodded his head, giving his gunmen the signal, and shots rang out as bullet after bullet ripped through Tical's body, jerking him left and right each time a bullet hit him. Tical never let Nautica's body go as he got filled with holes.

Once the smoke cleared, Tical and his woman lay dead in a pool of blood together, with over one hundred shell casings scattered on the floor. In death they eloped forever.

Questions for Book Discussion

Questions for Book Discussion

1. Did the story end the way you expected it to?
2. Do you think Nautica got what she deserved in the last chapter?
3. If you were Tical, would you have given Nautica another chance after learning about all the lies and deceit?
4. Who was your favorite character? Why?
5. Did Loon really love Nautica?
6. Who was a better fit for Tical, Millie or Nautica?
7. Imagine you are in Nautica's shoes and Loon approaches you with the threat of blackmail. How would you handle it?
8. Who was more your type, Tical or Zion? And why? For men, Millie or Nautica?
9. Would you like to read a sequel focused on Millie?

*Special shout-out to Coast2Coast readers, Reading Rendezvous, and OOSA online book clubs.

Please contact the author and tell your views and opinions at:

Quavo_writer@yahoo.com
Or
www.myspace.com/quavo_writer1